MW00942425

Perilous Passage

A Novel of Mystery and Adventure

PJ Dischino

with Sara Dischino

DEDICATION

To Grandmothers and Granddaughters,
a perfect combination

CONTENTS

ACKNOWLEDGMENTS

Thanks to my friends in my writing group who encouraged me to fulfill my dream from day one: Marie Edelen, JoAnn Shipman, Judy Lopez, and Hannah Miron. Leslie Lightfoot, Judy Ralph, and Laura Rausch, although newcomers to our writing group, gave valuable additional assistance.

Forever gratitude to my editor, Cynthia Krejcsi, without whom I could not have fulfilled my dream.
And special thanks to my husband, Joe, for his encouragement, love, and support.
.

1 HAPPY BIRTHDAY SARA

Sara's birthday started out being pretty predictable—at least as predictable as any of hers had ever been. On August 2, she woke up around 7:00 a.m., early for her. Summer sleeping habits preclude any activity before 11:00 a.m. However, birthdays require you to be awake to enjoy every minute. After all, you have to wait 364 days until the next one!

The first greeting of the morning was from her dad. He was really big on birthdays. To him, birthdays were holidays from normal routines. If your birthday fell on a workday, you took the day off. If it fell on a school day, you played hooky. Her birthday didn't fit into either category, so she was out of luck there.

Those once-a-year celebrations were always a day to remember, thanks to her parents. Sara was told that her first birthday was a zinger. There were pictures galore to prove it. Tents, clowns, blown-up slides, and jumping equipment were all brought in to celebrate this gala occasion. Driving instructions were announced on the radio. You have to agree that was some blast! It would have been nice if she remembered it, though.

Her birthdays were always kept special, so today she

loved the idea that fun things were planned. Mom, Dad, AJ, Gram, and Grandpa, along with her best friend, Samantha, were going to "Joe's" for dinner. Afterward, they would attend the Paper Mill Playhouse to see the musical *Into the Woods*.

Taking a long look at her reflection in the bathroom mirror was not unpleasant. Her naturally brown hair had been highlighted with soft red streaks. The effects pleased her—certainly worth the verbal battle with her mom, who was not in favor of this grown-up venture. Sara thought it added a bit of sophistication to her petite size, not her favorite attribute. All of her friends were adding inches to their height. She was stuck at five foot one. Even though she was slim, she envied the tall, willowy look. Adding another birthday did not magically add another inch.

The birthday girl was looking forward to a good time. The entire day stretched out before her, giving her a warm glow.

She was glad to be spending time with Samantha. Since Sara and her family had moved to another town in New Jersey, she hadn't been able to see Samantha very often, even though the driving distance wasn't all that far. They texted every day, but that wasn't the same as being together. This evening would be a great time to catch up on missed news.

There were several reasons why Samantha was such a good friend. First of all, she was loyal and never petty. Second, they had a similar sense of humor; it was not unusual for the two friends to have laughing fits over the least little event that might seem weird to others. And finally, Sara didn't even remember if they ever argued. Although Sara was often critical of people, she and Samantha melded perfectly.

Joe's was the best spot to enjoy Italian food. Well, maybe Italy ranks #1. Dinner there had to be fun. Laughing and slurping clams with red sauce couldn't be beat.

The Paper Mill Playhouse usually put on an excellent performance considering its proximity to Manhattan. The show, *Into the Woods*, was familiar, although Sara had never seen it in total. She played a character from that production last year at a dramatic arts camp. "Children Will Listen" was a beautiful song from the play, and she sang it as a solo. Everyone was full of compliments and said she did a beautiful job. Sara silently agreed with them. The theater, particularly musicals, was her passion.

Today looked good.

As Sara predicted, time passed pleasantly. Dinner turned out to be delicious, as usual. Joe and Annette, the restaurant owners, topped the meal by delivering a huge vanilla-iced cake with 15 sputtering candles to their table. All kinds of wishes were scrolled with edible words between the candles. Not only traditional birthday wishes covered the cake, but distinctive phrases meant for her alone added to the decorations. Dad had used his special name for her since she was a baby, "Happy Birthday Spunda Bear." Mom followed with "Happy Birthday to the best daughter in the world." Her younger brother, AJ, had a unique and funny message, "YppaH YadhtriB AraS." Gram and Grandpa's prediction was a bit mysterious, "Your 15th year may lead to adventure." Samantha's contribution was a simple "Happy Birthday Sara, Samantha."

Between the pasta and the dessert, Sara opened her perfect presents. Her hints had hit the right ears: six months of voice lessons from Mom and Dad, the coolest shirt from Samantha, and a candle shaped like Aladdin's lamp from AJ. They had all heard her requests for the past month. Nothing like getting your order in early!

Suddenly it was time to leave for the show. Sara was getting a bit antsy. Grandpa was sipping his coffee as if it were a bottomless cup.

"Come on, Grandpa. It's show time."

She hoped this would move the party to the next event.

He continued sipping, but something was happening. Slowly, a broad grin spread from ear to ear, and he began laughing.

"Didn't you expect something from us to mark the occasion—a little memento to show you have reached another rung on the age ladder?" he mused.

"We usually don't forget you," Gram chimed in, her smile equaling Grandpa's.

Sara knew something was up. Getting to the theater was now on pause. Her grandparents' presents were often completely unexpected. Others in the party seemed to be more aware of what was going on. Her curiosity soared. Thankfully, the answer was forthcoming.

Grandpa began by announcing, "Next week, Gram and I are going to Europe on the Celebrity Cruise Line. We're sailing on their ship named 'Serenade.' Rome and Gaeta are on our itinerary; then we will return to Rome, stay overnight, and take an early-morning flight back home. All this will take over two weeks."

Gram finished with "Do you think you would like to join us?"

SILENCE! MORE SILENCE! GULP.

Sara managed to find her voice. "Oh, oh that is fantastic! Of course I would love to go."

The thunderbolt had hit! She hoped her answer and expression conveyed her overwhelming excitement and appreciation. This would make a classic answer when anyone asked what she had done on her summer vacation.

Everyone was smiling, except for AJ. Gram noted his crestfallen expression. She tried to brighten his mood by saying his time would come for a special gift when he was a little older.

"How much older?"

Everyone laughed. AJ, at ten years of age, was not one for subtleties. No one had an appropriate response. Answers were full of generalities. Sara empathized with him and promised to bring back a "wow" present for him.

It was all settled. They were to board the Celebrity Cruise ship "Serenade" on August 9. There would be a lot to do during the next week. These were chores with a purpose, and that purpose was in a folder called ADVENTURE!

The play was wonderful, and every tune played straight to her heart. It had been the perfect ending to a perfect birthday, and Sara was on a high. She had often spent time with her grandparents. They had lived in South Carolina for a number of years, offering Sara a wonderful vacation mecca. At five years of age, she had gone for a visit, flying alone from Newark Airport in New Jersey to Charleston, South Carolina. She had established independence even at that age! Now that her grandparents had moved back to New Jersey and were living close by, they were there with her and for her. Gram and Grandpa were warm and caring and, for being from a totally different generation, very with it.

You are probably coming to the conclusion that life had dealt Sara a pretty nice hand. No one can argue that fact. Of course, it wasn't all picture perfect. If you think this trip will be a continuation of high notes, you are in for a surprise!

2 THE BEST-LAID PLANS

Days flew by as Sara, Gram, and Grandpa organized their travel plans. There was shopping, validating her passport, shopping, checking her basic needs, shopping, a hair salon appointment, and everything else needed to complete travel requirements. Oh—was shopping mentioned? Sara packed and repacked at least two dozen times. To her, going to Europe was like going into outer space. She worried that she might desperately need something and there would be no place to purchase it. "Best be prepared" was her new motto.

Based on the brochure, the amenities on board looked fabulous. It seemed like Paradise. What really blew her away was a photo of a stateroom with outside glass walls. It looked like you were walking on water. Just picture brushing your teeth in a setting like that!

On August 8, one day shy of D Day (also known as Departure Day), they had to take care of a few last-minute details like a trip to the orthodontist's to fix a broken wire and pick up wax. She was supposed to have the braces removed, but the specialist wanted to delay that for a few months. Having to wear braces on this fantastic trip was so gross! Verizon was next on the list. Grandpa wanted to check on phones, making sure they would work in Europe.

When they had completed all their tasks, AJ asked if he could go to practice at the batting cages. A unanimous "yes" rang out. Since poor AJ was out of the "trip circle," it was great to do something just for him. Dad, Sara, Grandpa, and Gram went along to cheer him on.

There was a crowd at the batting cages, so they had a bit of a wait. At last AJ found himself in his favorite position, behind a bat. For two hours he was right in his element. When it was time to leave, Gram, Grandpa, and Sara left the batting cages first. AJ and Dad wanted to stay a few more minutes.

As they were walking to their car, Sara saw two bike riders chasing each other. They weren't paying attention to their surroundings as they raced in and out of the parking spaces, trying to outmaneuver each other.

As they came closer to her, Sara leaped to avoid a collision. Grandpa was not so lucky. He was opening the car door when catastrophe struck. Grandpa and the bicycle collided. The force knocked him against the open car door and then onto the ground. The offending bicycle and its rider were sprawled several feet away.

AJ and Dad got there just in time to see it happen. AJ ran over to the offender with bat in hand, ready to use it as a weapon. Dad quickly disarmed him by grabbing the bat.

Grandpa was obviously in great pain, so Dad called 911. When the EMS aids and firemen arrived, they determined that Grandpa needed to be taken directly to the nearest hospital. Gram sat at his side in the ambulance while everyone else followed them to the hospital in Grandpa's car.

The police notified the bicyclists' parents to go directly to the hospital. The boys knew they were in for a rough time as the police car drove to the hospital, and their former bravado quickly turned to dread.

It was a forlorn group assembled in St. Joseph's waiting room. Angry parents glared at their wayward sons. Their faces ash white with fear, the boys sat listening as the police brought their parents up to date. They knew the severity of their punishment would depend on how badly Grandpa had been hurt. Gram was still with Grandpa, but the other family members sat anxiously awaiting news. They had no idea how extensive his injuries were.

A few hours later, Gram came down the hall talking to a tall woman in a white coat. Dr. Renzel introduced herself and said her specialty was orthopedic surgery. After examining Grandpa and looking at his X-rays, she was happy to say that he would not need surgery. However, he had two broken ribs and would have to keep his shoulder immobilized. Although he would be released from the hospital today, recovery time and therapy eliminated any travel plans for at least six months.

Everyone was grateful that Grandpa would recover. Everything else was unimportant. Before leaving with their sons, the mothers of the two boys made sure they apologized. Grandpa explained the aftermath of what they had done to the two trembling boys. Not only had he been painfully injured but they had ruined all thoughts of a delightful adventure. Plans had been destroyed because of their thoughtlessness. Tears welled up in the culprits' eyes.

His point made, Grandpa softened his tone. "I'm sure you realize the damage you've caused by your thoughtlessness. I just hope you've learned how important it is to think before trying an activity that might look like fun but could be dangerous to you or to someone else."

The two chagrined young men assured Grandpa they had indeed learned a valuable lesson. Then their fuming parents steered them out of the hospital. The boys hadn't heard the last of it, though. As it turned out, they had to meet with a judge, who admonished them about their irresponsibility and told them how lucky they were that Grandpa had decided not to press charges. Thanks to him, they wouldn't have anything on their permanent record. However, the judge still assigned them to do community service every weekend for the next two months.

3 ALL IS NOT LOST

It was an even sadder troop that gathered at Sara's grandparents' house that evening. Everyone's first concern was making sure Grandpa was as comfortable as possible. The patient wanted to be part of the family conversation, but he agreed to lie down on the couch. He started out by suggesting that perhaps someone else might accompany Gram and Sara on the trip. Gram tried to squelch that idea by refusing to leave him for that length of time.

"Oh come on. I'm not that disabled. I just can't travel. Kim or Kirk could look in on me and pick up what I need," he insisted. "Or better yet, maybe Kim can take my place."

Sara's Aunt Kim, who lived a few miles away, had rushed to the hospital when she heard what had happened and was with them when they brought Grandpa home several hours later. Sara's Uncle Kirk, who lived farther away, had just arrived.

A pained look crossed Aunt Kim's face. "Oh, I would love that, but I can't go away next week. We have a big gymnastic competition, and as head coach I have to be there. But I can certainly stay with Dad."

The conversation went back and forth, but they

couldn't find a solution. Grandpa's pain pills had kicked in by now. He was fighting sleep because he didn't want to miss anything, but with a comfortable pillow and cover enveloping him, he began to doze off between bits of their conversation.

Sara was already resigned to disappointment when Gram expressed a new thought. "You know, there is the possibility of Sara and me going by ourselves. We already have drivers, tour guides, and all kinds of help lined up. If Sara doesn't mind traveling with one old lady, I'm up to it, if it's all right with our wounded Joe."

Grandpa woke up when his name was mentioned. When they told him what he had missed, his eyes brightened. "Great idea! Let's call Brian, our travel agent, and see what he thinks."

Suddenly the world looked a little brighter. Gram might be of a totally different generation, but Sara always enjoyed her company. The old adage "Where there's a will, there's a way" really held true. Gram was full of those old sayings. Sara often had no idea what they meant, but this one was right on target.

Brian expressed concern for Grandpa, hoping for a speedy recovery. He assured them that Gram's idea was feasible and said he would contact the cruise line and the hotels right away to find out how they might further accommodate Gram and Sara. In less than an hour he called them back to say that a representative from the Celebrity Line would be calling them soon. As previously planned, hotel personnel would be there to meet them at various train stations. In Rome, they would be picked up at the ship terminal for transportation to the hotel.

Ten minutes later, the Celebrity Cruise Line called. Gram put the call on speaker phone so everybody could hear the conversation. A man speaking with a formal British accent expressed his concern for their situation. He suggested that instead of returning the money for Grandpa's ticket, the Celebrity Line could have a special assistant assigned to make sure all of Gram and Sara's needs would be addressed from their arrival onboard until the end of their trip. The arrangement also included seating at the Captain's table as well as upgraded cabins.

Grandpa, now fully awake, smiled for the first time since his accident. Gram accepted, thanking the representative for the generous offer. He said it was his pleasure to be of assistance and wished the travelers "Bon Voyage."

As soon as Gram hung up, she said, "Joe, I cannot believe it. Do you know how much that is worth? Only wealthy or V.I.P. customers get that kind of treatment. Even though you're not going to be able to enjoy the trip, your family certainly will!"

4 HOLD THE SHIP

Sara was filled with mixed emotions. She had so much admiration for her grandparents and the way they handled events. All her family was so supportive. But she was a bit anxious about how this trip would unfold since everything had been solved on the spur of the moment.

Little did Sara know then what fate had in store for her and Gram. If she had been privy to the future, a little nervousness would have been the least of her concerns!

5 DO YOU HAVE YOUR PASSPORT?

D Day had arrived. It was finally August 9. The whole family, except for Grandpa, was going to brunch at the Tabboon Restaurant, which was right near the Manhattan cruise terminal where they would board. At this point, Sara just wanted to be on the ship. It was hard to join the light-hearted conversation whirling around her. Her thoughts were with Grandpa, wishing she could make all evidence of his accident vanish. She knew Gram was thinking the same thing. Hopefully, once they got on board, the uniqueness of a different setting would help to soften their sadness.

The trip to the dock took no time. Dad parked the car as close to the terminal as possible and began unloading their mound of luggage. Sara definitely out-bagged Gram. All that shopping had resulted in a plethora (Sara loved that word.) of luggage.

Suddenly it was actually time to board. As they entered the terminal, they spotted a tall young gentleman holding a sign with their name. As they walked up to him, he asked, "Are you the Dischino passengers?"

"Yes, we are!"

"Great! Let me introduce myself. I am Travis

Hemsfield, and I am with the Celebrity Cruise Line."

Travis was there to assist them with registration and boarding, so it was time to say goodbye to the family. They all exchanged hugs, a little tighter than normal. AJ even clung to Sara, much to her surprise. She began to think this kid who was often such a pain was actually going to miss her.

After getting a "red cap" to load their luggage onto a large dolly, Travis asked them for their tickets and passports and motioned them to follow him. As Sara walked away from her family, she glanced back at those beloved faces with warmth and a bit of nostalgia. Then a wave of pleasant expectancy took over.

Formalities took less time than they had expected. Soon they each had a card that was to be used for all their needs while onboard. Neither cash nor credit cards were accepted on the ship.

Finally, the two travelers boarded the magnificent ship. Its mission and theirs were simpatico: pure enjoyment was the name of the game.

6 READY, SET, SAIL

Travis suggested they have something to eat, take some time to look around, or just relax while he had their luggage delivered to their cabin. At noon they were to meet him at the ship's concierge desk on Deck 7, where he would introduce them to the personal guide who would be responsible for their well-being.

Gram and Sarah agreed that a brief tour was a good choice. With a deck plan in hand, they were off to see some of the huge ship's offerings. They laughed about the umpteen times they would probably get lost. The ship held 10,000 passengers and had 12 decks. Sara carried her card in a new bag that could either be used as a shoulder strap purse or, by shortening the straps, as a belt with a purse attached, leaving her hands free. Her mom found it online and gave it to her as a bon voyage present from Dad, AJ, and her. Pretty cool! Sara had it loaded up, and since she was using it as a shoulder bag, it was pretty hefty.

Sara and Gram decided to look at the pools first. Two indoor and three outdoor giant glistening glories tempted passengers to include pool time on their schedules. One even had simulated waves to compete with the Atlantic! Gram said she hoped there would be some young people among the predominately senior population on the ship. Sara assured her that even if there weren't, it wouldn't be a problem given all that the ship had to offer.

Noting that it was almost noon, the two set out to meet Travis at the hospitality desk. Several wrong turns cost them time and frustration before they saw their destination. Travis saw them and motioned for them to join him.

Sara lost sight of Travis as she maneuvered through the crowd that had formed in front of the concierge desk. Unfortunately, that was her down-fall—literally! In her hurry, she didn't notice the backpack on the floor; but when her shoe got caught in its strap, she went flying. Suddenly she was no longer standing upright but sprawled out on her stomach, smashed against the hard surface of a tile floor.

7 THE FALL THAT BROUGHT THEM TOGETHER

It took a few seconds to realize what had happened. With her eyes closed, Sara tried to assess the damage. Generally, she hurt all over; but specifically, her leg throbbed. As she slowly opened her eyes, two doll-sized white Mary Jane shoes popped up in front of her. Lifting up her head to widen her range of vision, she focused on the body of a small girl attached to the Mary Janes.

The child was bending over her with an expression of concern and curiosity. "Does your booboo hurt?"

Given the blood all over Sara's clothes, Miss Mary Jane's question was very logical.

Travis and Gram were by her side in an instant. Gram was wearing the same expression she had when Grandpa was hurt. The little girl had several concerned companions with her, including a few adults and a boy around Sara's age. As people gathered around her, Sara's number one emotion was embarrassment.

Luckily, the wounds were superficial. With some assistance, Sara found herself sitting in a comfortable chair. Ten minutes later, the ship's doctor had cleaned and bandaged her cuts, but her feeling of discomfort at being the center of attention as well as a klutz remained.

The boy who was with Miss Mary Jane's group kneeled down by her chair.

"I'm so sorry. This is all my fault. That was my backpack you tripped over. I should never have left it there."

"He's certainly right. We are so sorry!" a woman's voice chimed in. Sara assumed it belonged to the boy's mother.

A group of six seemingly related bodies, as well as Travis, Gram, and the doctor, surrounded the fallen traveler. Sara smiled weakly, hoping to deflate their anxiety. Now that the doctor had determined her injuries were minor, Sara just wanted to get to her cabin. She certainly did not want to be the center of attention so early in the game—especially under these circumstances. The doctor asked her to stand and walk a bit, which she was able to do. Everyone was relieved.

Moments later, a pretty dark-haired lady with an engaging smile walked up to them. Travis said, "This is Siobhan Ennis. She is the ship's personal guide who has been assigned to you and your grandmother. I am placing you in her care now as I have to leave the ship before it sails. I'm sorry your trip began the way it did, but hopefully this beautiful ship and all she has to offer will make up for it."

They thanked Travis for all his help and then, with a warm wave, he was off.

Siobhan charmed Gram and Sara with her warm Irish smile and voice, assuring them she would do her best to make their ocean voyage smooth sailing.

"Your room and luggage are all ready. If you will follow me, I will escort you to your cabin. Are you up to it, Sara?" Siobhan's thick Irish accent made the request sound delightful.

The people they passed on the way must have thought Gram and Sara were celebrities, given all the personal attention Sara was receiving. Little did they know how "average" they really were.

Before they got to their room, they met the parents of the boy with the backpack. After apologizing once again, they asked, "How about meeting us in the Outrigger Salon on the Lido Deck at 4:00 to watch the ship get underway? We'll order champagne to celebrate the voyage."

Gram and Sara graciously accepted the invitation. Meeting late in the afternoon would give everyone time to get settled in and acclimated to their environs.

Their cabin was Number 623 on Deck 6. Siobhan unlocked the door, and they stepped into their beautifully appointed quarters. These were some digs! The furniture had been arranged to give each of them as much privacy as possible. The twin beds, chests, and tables were well positioned, leaving plenty of room to move around. A dining table welcomed them with a display of lovely flowers, a bottle of wine, glasses, and a bowl of fruit.

Whoever designed ship staterooms got it right. There was plenty of storage, and even Sarah was able to put all of her belongings away. The bathroom was cleverly designed with shelves, cabinets, and drawers that accommodated all of their makeup and other necessities. Once again, Sara's thoughts went to Grandpa. He would have loved this ship.

8 GREAT DIGS

Sara said, "This place is gorgeous. Did you expect it to be so splendid, Gram?"

"We had chosen an upgraded stateroom, but this is above and beyond. I didn't know a balcony was included. This must be part of the changes they included in our special upgrade," Gram added.

A knock on the door interrupted their musings. Siobhan came in with a clipboard in hand. She immediately asked Sara how she felt. Amazingly, Sara realized she hadn't thought about her fall for a while. She felt fine and was ready to go.

This charming young lady had the warmest of smiles. She breezed through her announcements, telling them that dinner was at 6:00 and they would be seated at the Captain's table. After placing a copy of the itinerary for that night and the next day's activities on the desk, she pointed to the phone and said that if they needed anything they could get in touch with her by dialing 8.

After Siobhan left, Sara looked over the daily newsletters. One of the pages was specifically for children and teenagers. She would read that more carefully later. Now it was time to explore!

They visited the theater and were amazed at its enormous size. The variety of programs that were offered was impressive, so enjoying the entertainment every night would definitely go on their "must do" list.

They were on their way to check out the computer room when they realized it was time to get ready for their first social event. They needed time to change into something more formal as dinner at the Captain's table would probably follow right after their celebration with their new acquaintances.

Sharing one bathroom proved a bit time consuming, but they were still decked out in their finery by 3:45. They exchanged compliments with each other on their dress selections, and then off they went. It was a good thing they had a little time to spare because it took a bit of meandering to find the Outrigger Salon.

There were several directories on each deck, something to help them navigate from then on. Fellow passengers were all familiarizing themselves with their temporary home. At every turn there was something new to discover. As they entered the salon, the bouncy little girl with the Mary Janes ran up to them and threw her arms around Sara's legs. She really was a cutie.

"Hurry, we found seats right by a big, big, big window. We can see the dock. Soon the ship will leave and we will be on a big, big, big ocean!" She was jumping up and down as she encouraged them to move faster, drawing them closer to her family.

A woman whom Sara assumed was "Miss Enthusiasm's" mother rose quickly from her seat to greet them. "Martha is so excited about everything that has to do with the ship. I was afraid she was about to cause another spill for you. How are you? Come join us."

Sara wasn't thrilled hearing about her nose dive again, but she understood the woman's concern and reported that all was fine.

"Oh that's so good to hear."

9 WHO ARE THESE PEOPLE?

Everyone else at the table stood up to greet them, and Sara took the opportunity to try to figure out their relationship. There was an older couple, probably in their 70s, like her grandmother. Another couple seemed closer to her parents' age. Then there was a really nerdy boy, shorter than she was, with thick dark-rimmed glasses and a preppie shirt that most of the boys she knew would never wear. He was the owner of that killer backpack. The little energetic bundle of a girl completed the family.

Hoping they wouldn't think of her as just a klutz if she did something mature, Sara decided to begin the introductions. Leaving the comfort of the outer circle, Sara stepped toward the middle of the group, hoping to pull this off.

"I'm Sara Dischino and this is my Grandmother, Pat," she said, extending her hand to the closest person. She assumed he was the father.

"Pleasure to meet you, Sara. I wish we had started out in a different way. I'm Martin Balsalm. This is my wife, Leanne, my mother and father, George and Anne Balsalm, our daughter, Martha, and Lincoln, our son. Let's sit down and get acquainted."

They sat down at a large round table, which was a great way to see and be seen. Everyone in the family seemed so personable, even Lincoln. Unfortunately, not only was he nerdy, but so was his name.

"The waiter is bringing the champagne. Sara, what would you like to drink?" asked George Balsam.

She asked for ice tea with lemon, hoping that it didn't sound unworldly. As their drinks arrived, a loud blast from the ship's horn signaled that the voyagers were about to get their sea legs. As the ship left Manhattan, conversations began to fill in gaps about each other's worlds. Martha entered the dialogue by stating that she was very hungry. That remark made them realize they were all hungry too.

10 UPSCALE DINING

It turned out that they were all were dining at the Captain's table. Sara was really pleased. Even though Lincoln was not her type (She really hadn't determined what her type was, but Lincoln didn't even come close.), during their brief conversation she was happy to discover that he had a sense of humor.

They were just about to leave the salon and search for the dining hall and the Captain's table when a man approached them. He was around Sara's father's age and had red hair that was definitely out of a bottle!

Introducing himself as Simon Kellar, he began speaking to Lincoln's grandfather. "I was told that you are going to Rome to join the new ambassador's staff. I will be part of the attaché at the embassy. I hope we can spend some time getting acquainted while we're onboard the ship."

"Perhaps later, but right now we are on the way to enjoy our first dinner," replied George Balsalm, offering a weak smile to Simon.

Simon quickly picked up on this lukewarm response. "Well, it was a pleasure meeting you, sir. Enjoy dinner."

In a few minutes he was out sight. Sara was happy

about that, since there was something bothersome about him. She didn't think she was the only one who felt that way either.

Simon quickly vanished from Sara's thoughts as they tried to solve the puzzle of reaching the Captain's table. But she needn't have worried, because when they entered the dining hall, Siobhan greeted them.

"Good evening, Mrs. Dischino and Sara. Please allow me to take you to the Captain's table." Recognizing the rest of the group, Siobhan greeted them with her warm Gaelic smile.

The Captain's table was a sight to behold. Gleaming place settings for 12 beckoned them to be seated. Their group occupied eight chairs. Gram was seated on one side of Sara while Lincoln sat on her other side. Shortly after they were seated, the Captain arrived, along with his Staff Captain. She learned later that it's the role of the Staff Captain to deal with every onboard activity and conflict. As they exchanged introductions, out of the corner of her eye Sara saw Simon walk by their table and wave at George. As far as she could determine, the wave was not returned. Simon quickly vanished into the sea of passengers.

11 BONDING

Dinner went even better than Sara had anticipated. She was able to find out quite a bit about Lincoln and his family. For instance, Lincoln preferred to be called Linc. He'd been unhappy with that creepy name since forever. All the male members of the Balsalm family were named after American presidents: George (Washington), Martin (Van Buren), and Lincoln. And Miss Twinkle Toes, Martha, was named after President Washington's wife. Both George and his son were history buffs, so Sara discovered that her honors history classes were paying off sooner than expected.

As it turned out, George was not part of the new Italian ambassador's attaché. He *was* the Ambassador. However, for security reasons he wanted it kept secret while they were onboard. Now Sara understood Mr. Balsalm's reluctance to have much of a discussion with Simon. If Simon were authentic, wouldn't he know more about the Ambassador? Sara thought there was indeed something odd about the man.

The Captain had a foreign accent that Sara couldn't quite place. He was a tall, distinguished-looking man and had the bluest eyes. He also possessed an ease with conversation that enabled him to bring out the interests of everyone at the table, making each person feel special. It was obvious to Sara that the Captain had hosted such dinners repeatedly over the years. Nobody monopolized the conversation. Everyone had a humorous story to tell. No part of the conversation was too serious.

Gram apologized to Sara for relating a tale she'd heard many times before, but it was a great car story and Gram was the perfect storyteller. She had no trouble holding everyone's interest as the story unfolded.

Gram had been a teacher for 25 years. One bitter January morning on her way to school, she remembered that she had to pick up 12 copies of the *New York Times*. That day each student in her gifted class would be assigned to pick a journalist with a byline, read an article written by the reporter, highlight the important points, and then summarize it for the rest of the class. The following week, students who worked on the school newspaper would visit the *Times* newsrooms.

She decided the best place to purchase the papers was at a coffee shop that also sold newspapers and magazines. She left the car running while she ran inside to get the papers. After all, how many car thieves are lurking about in ten degree weather? The purchase took only a few minutes, and she was back in the car on her way to school.

After driving a few miles, she had a feeling something was not quite right. Then she noticed two baby shoes swinging merrily away from the rearview mirror.

"Oh, this isn't my car! I've taken someone else's car. The other driver must have left the motor running too." During the bitter cold weather, it wasn't unusual for drivers to let their car idle while they ran into a shop to pick something up.

Making a fast U-turn and driving as if the police were after her, Gram returned to the "scene of the crime." There was her car, with the engine still running. No one was in sight, so she quickly parked the "stolen" vehicle, jumped into her own car, and sped away.

After a few minutes, the same feeling returned. She looked down at the seat next to her and saw an unfamiliar brown bag. "Oh, now I've taken the other driver's lunch."

Another fast U-turn got Gram back to the coffee shop in a few minutes. Not a soul was on the street, but luckily the car was still there. She opened the door, threw the brown bag on the seat, and sped off. She had committed the perfect crime!

Gram laughed all the way to school. She couldn't wait to tell everyone about her adventure. About an hour after she arrived, an announcement came over the loud speaker: "Please be advised that the local police have had recent complaints about car and lunch thefts. Do not leave your car with the engine running or you may lose your car and your lunch too!" Her colleagues were certainly having fun over her bizarre behavior!

After they finished dinner, Gram and Sara and the Balsalms decided to see the 8:30 show. That turned out to be a great idea because they really enjoyed the magician, who performed the most unbelievable act. No one could figure out the secret to his illusion. At the end of the show, everyone felt beat. Nine o'clock breakfast in the dining hall seemed a great time and place to start their second day.

In their room, Gram and Sara took some time to rehash events. Sara tried to write about what had transpired since they set sail. After a few paragraphs, writing became a chore while the bed beckoned to her. The gentle rocking motion of the ship provided a natural aide to sleep.

12 WHAT WAS THAT ALL ABOUT?

On day two, a good morning announcement from the Captain awakened them, reminding them where they were while presenting the new passengers with a multitude of options on how to spend their day. They also realized that they better move quickly if they wanted to join their new friends for breakfast. It would take a bit of maneuvering considering there was only one bathroom.

Gram and Sara took time to look over the ship's daily bulletins. Gram's bulletin was different from Sara's; it listed activities that would appeal to adults. Gram emphasized that if anything on Sara's bulletin appealed to her, she should do it. There were programs that sounded like fun. Sara thought she would ask Linc to join her. He had moved way up in Sara's opinion because he was funny and very friendly. The wave simulation pool sounded awesome. Little Miss Jumping Bean, Martha, would love that.

Gram read the descriptions of several pursuits that sounded interesting to her. "Anne and Leanne Balsalm had mentioned doing a few things, but I certainly don't want to impose on them. If they suggest I join them something, that's fine. Just sitting on the deck reading a good book sounds inviting to me, though. I'll play it by ear."

Breakfast with their new friends was a continuation of the pleasure they enjoyed the previous evening. The Balsalms were turning into congenial travel companions. Plans came up in conversations about the day. Anne, looking at Gram, talked about a few events they might enjoy. She also asked if everyone would like to eat at 6:00 again. That left time to see the show afterwards. It was obvious they were including the newcomers.

It was quite understandable that Sara's grandmother did not want them to become "tag alongs" of their new friends. She was adamant in making the Balsalms aware of this. She told Anne, "Sara and I hope you don't feel you have to include us. You are a family and might just want to dine alone. We don't want to interfere with any of your plans."

The Balsalm family assured them over and over that they enjoyed their new friends and wanted to spend more time with them. All agreed to choose activities separately or with each other; but if activities worked out for them as a group, then that would be a plus.

As they left the dining room, Gram and Sara decided to go back to their room before starting their first activity. The others had the same idea.

"There's a program for Martha. I'll take her there and get her settled. Then I'll call your room, and we can decide where to meet. Does that work for you, Pat?" Leanne asked.

"Sounds perfect."

Linc and Sara decided to meet at the Teen Lounge in an hour.

Their paths separated quickly but only temporarily. Everyone was anticipating nothing but good times ahead.

Never assume!

Halfway back to their room, Gram said, "Oh Sara, I forgot my sweater in the dining hall. I'm going back to pick it up. Why don't you go back to the room? I'll be right there."

Sara decided to go back to the dining hall with her. They turned around quickly and obviously unexpectedly, for they nearly tripped over Simon. There was no question in their minds that he had been following them.

"Oh hi, Mrs. Dischino. Hi, Sara. It's nice to see you. Are you enjoying your trip so far?" he inquired.

They answered "yes" and then moved on, wondering why he was always entering the picture. He knew their names even though they had never been introduced. An uncomfortable feeling clouded the moment. Something odd and unpleasant was going on.

With a puzzled expression, Sara said, "That sure was weird!" She was voicing the concern both of them were feeling at that moment. Gram's facial expression showed complete agreement. Neither wanted to dwell on the incident, though, so they retrieved the sweater and then went back to the room before carrying on with their separate plans.

13 NEVER A DULL MOMENT

Linc was waiting for Sara outside the Teen Lounge. Before she got there, he had already checked out everything the lounge had to offer. "This place looks awesome," he told her. "They have a lounge deck set aside for teens that's close to the pool with the wave simulator, karaoke nights, video games galore—a lot of neat stuff."

They walked inside together and looked around. Linc was right. There was a variety of options—something for everyone. Sara stopped for a minute to get the total picture and noticed another girl about her age reading a bulletin pinned to the corkboard on the wall. She wore a blue-and-white-striped bikini and was still toweling off water droplets after her dip in the pool.

"You look like you've been swimming," Sara said, hoping to sound friendly.

The girl turned to see who was talking to her. She was excited to see a girl her age with a friendly smile. "Oh hi. Yes, the pool is great. You almost feel like you're at the beach. I'm Katherine Delvin. I love this whole teen set up."

The two girls talked for several minutes. Katherine mentioned that there was going to be a pool party with a disco that night around 10:00, right after the show. It sounded like it would be a blast. Sara agreed that it did sound awesome but mentioned she didn't know what her group was planning for the evening. They decided to exchange room numbers so they could reconnect later.

"Nice meeting you, Katherine. Maybe we'll see each other at the pool party or later on in the day."

"Cool, Sara. That would be fun."

Sara looked for Linc so that she could introduce him to Katherine, but he was nowhere to be found. She noticed a door leading to a nearby pool and decided to see if that's where he had gone. As soon as she opened the door, she held her ears. The shouts of people getting slapped by the simulated wave were almost deafening.

She scanned the area and finally spotted Linc. "There you are! I couldn't find you. Why did you disappear?"

Linc hung his head, trying to hide the sheepish look on his face. After pausing a moment, he replied, "Sara, you don't need me hanging around all the time. You are really terrific in every way. There are lots of other kids for you to meet here, and you'll probably have more in common with them than you do with me—like the girl you were just talking with. I've never been very popular, and I don't want you to be stuck with me."

As soon as Linc finished his brief soliloquy, Sara jumped right in. "You have it all wrong. Let's get something straight. You certainly don't have a good image of yourself. You are great to be with. You're easy to get along with—funny, kind, smart. I enjoy your company. And I don't care who is popular and who isn't."

Sara pointed to a nearby table with two chairs and suggested that they sit down and talk. A waiter came by to tell them about the teen cocktails. He asked if they would like to order anything. The drinks had familiar names but didn't contain any alcohol. Linc relaxed and ordered a Mean Martini. Sara knew she had made her point and ordered a Mojo Mojito.

During the next hour she and Linc discovered quite a bit about each other. Sara explained how her grandparents' birthday gift became a reality, described her grandfather's accident, and shared everything else leading up to their boarding the ship. She admitted that her economic status was average and middle class and that the cruise line had given her and Gram the upgraded cabin when Grandpa couldn't go with them.

She was, as Linc had guessed, popular in school. Sara felt it was because she was open and basically friendly. Gossiping was not a quality that appealed to her. She admitted that at times she could be overly critical, though, so it took a lot for someone to be her close friend. On the other hand, loyalty was really important to her, and she appreciated the few really close friends she had.

Linc started with a brief family history. His great, great, great grandfather had been one of the Founding Fathers of the original Thirteen Colonies. He had established a paper mill that supplied printers with their paper. Sara hadn't known that paper was made from linen and cloth in colonial times. The following generations had carried on the business, improving and enlarging it until it became the largest paper supplier in the country. In recent years the company had also diversified into other types of businesses.

In spite of their wealth, the children certainly were not spoiled, and solid values had been passed down through the generations. But even though Linc's family had high standards, they were always supportive and loving. Respect for others as well as for material possessions was of paramount importance to them. Bragging to others about what they had was not tolerated. In addition, each generation had served its country.

Linc described his days at a private boys' school. He had a few good friends but thought that most students considered him socially inept, even a dork. He was average at best in sports and less than average with social communications. Getting top grades came easily, though, and he was privy to many historical and political discussions as his grandfathers and now his father were all in the political arena.

He had an older brother who was about to enter his senior year in college. Linc and Quincy (after Quincy Adams) were very close. Linc emailed him every day, keeping him up to date with every detail of the trip. Quincy was on his school's wrestling team and had to stay behind so that he could be at practice. However, he would join the family in Rome before they came back to the US. Right now he was staying at his other grandparents' house, and his college roommate was staying there with him. The roommate was a foreign exchange student and did not go home between semesters. Quincy and he had roomed together since they were freshman and now were close friends.

Linc also mentioned that he, Martha, and his parents were going to stay with his grandfather and grandmother at the Italian Embassy for three weeks and would fly home after that. Once again he urged her not to say anything about his grandfather's ambassadorship to anyone. Everything had to be "hush hush." Linc suspected something more was going on than his grandfather's appointment to ambassador. On the ship, the family was told to just say he will be an aide and to act natural. Really weird!

Sara felt that the two had reached a new level of friendship with this latest disclosure. Just as they were planning to meet in an hour by the pool, their discussion was interrupted by the walkie-talkie Sara carried in order to communicate with Gram while they were onboard the ship. Gram was just touching base.

"I think Linc and I are going to grab a bite in the Teen Salon. Then I'll go back to the cabin and put on my bathing suit. We are going to try out the Wave Simulator Pool. But I can always change plans if you have something else in mind," Sara told Gram.

"Oh no, Sara, go right ahead. I'm so happy you are enjoying yourself. Anne and Leanne are ordering salads and have asked me to join them in their suite, which I'll do now that I know you have your own plans. We'll all get together for dinner. How about if we connect around 5:00—or earlier, if necessary?"

"Sounds good to me. What did you do this morning?"

"Visited the shops. Sara, they have a lot to offer. And there are also stands with some very reasonably priced merchandise set up outside the stores. I bought a pretty scarf. This afternoon I'm going to the casino for about an hour to lose a little money. Oh, I got an email from Grandpa. He's feeling much better. Your aunt is taking good care of him. Our friends have been bringing him food galore so they certainly won't starve.

"That's pretty much all for now. Have fun, Baby Doll. I'll see you in a few hours."

14 AN UNPLEASANT EPISODE

Sara and Linc got a quick lunch and then arranged to meet again in a half hour. Sara couldn't wait to test the wave pool. As she walked toward the steps leading to deck 6, where her cabin was located, Sara had the uneasy feeling that she was being watched. The main salon was crowded with passengers rushing to their next activity. She had trouble sorting out anyone suspicious.

When she reached the stairs, a man suddenly stepped in from the outside deck and blocked her path. Sarah was frightened. She wanted to get as far away from him as possible.

The man grabbed Sara's wrist. "Hi, Sara. Are you enjoying your trip? Where's your sidekick, Linc?"

Her mouth went dry. When she finally was able to wrench her arm free, she heard someone calling her name. At first she couldn't tell where the voice was coming from. But when she heard her name called again, Sara turned to look up the stairs. As she did so, the assailant disappeared.

Looking down on her from the top of the stairs, Simon called out, "Sara, are you all right?"

"No, Simon, I'm not all right."

Within seconds, Simon was standing next to her. He

must have taken several steps at a time. In a few words, Sara told him about the man who had grabbed her. It was hard for her to talk (very unusual) since she was so upset. Simon said a few comforting words that created a calming atmosphere. Then he called her grandmother and Siobhan.

It was only a few minutes before a whole entourage surrounded them—led by Gram. Even her new friend, Katherine, was part of the group. Sara had to explain every detail of the encounter over and over.

Linc's grandfather was there too, and he was visibly shaken. He signaled to Simon, and the two men walked away together. Sara had no idea where they were going or what they were saying, but it looked like a pretty serious conversation.

Sara walked over to Katherine and asked her how she knew something was wrong.

"I called your room and your grandmother answered. She told me you were coming back to check emails and change for the pool, so I thought I would meet you at your room. I wanted to know if you were going to the show tonight. It's a comedy.

"When I got to your room, your grandmother was rushing out. She was very upset. She said there was a problem, but she didn't know what. She just told me to follow her."

Sara's next question was how everyone else got the news and got there so quickly. Gram replied that Simon must have contacted them. It turned out that she was right.

At that moment, George Balsam rejoined the group, his face lined with concern. "Sara, I'm so sorry this happened. Simon explained what little he had seen and heard. After hearing the story you related, I am at a loss as to why you were assaulted."

Sara replied, "Well, I'm not certain that the man meant to assault me. He disappeared when he heard Simon call my name, but the thought of what might have happened is frightening."

She was still shaking when Siobhan brought her a cup of hot tea and a sweater, telling her, "I'm going to keep you under my wing until we dock in Civitavecchia. You're a good skin."

They all smiled at Siobhan's Irish expression and her pert accent. The tea and the sweater felt comforting, and that scary feeling in the pit of Sara's stomach was diminishing. She realized there were many people who were watching out for her.

Noticing that Sara seemed calmer, George Balsalm put his hands on her shoulders and whispered, "Sara, I think we should meet in my suite in a half hour. I'll gather the rest of the family together, but please don't say *anything* to anybody except your grandmother." The *anything* was clearly emphasized.

As if on cue, Gram suggested, "Sara, let's go back to the room and relax for a while, maybe order room service."

"That's a great idea, Gram!"

15 CHANGING WINDS

It would be a relief getting out of the limelight. Sara couldn't wait to be alone with Gram to rehash events.

As they started to their cabin, Martha, with eyes as big as saucers, grabbed Sara's hand tightly. "I will stay with you and make sure no bad men get to you," she said solemnly.

"Thank you, honey. Don't worry. I will be fine. But I can tell you right now, you will be seeing a lot more of me," Sara said, trying to quell Martha's fears.

That seemed to work, for a smile replaced the serious expression on the child's face.

Sara suddenly realized she missed her own little brother. For all their sibling rivalry, he would have been there for her. She really missed him and that was weird.

As the group dispersed, Linc gave Sara a small wave. He looked worried too.

Sara made sure Gram and Siobhan were close by, which really wasn't necessary. They were not about to let her out of their sight.

The room looked so welcoming. After updating Gram about the meeting with George Balsalm, Sara flopped down on the bed and drifted off. She barely heard Siobhan ordering a snack from room service and Gram calling the Balsalm suite to change the meeting time. And finally she sank into a peaceful blackness.

16 PLOT AND FRIENDSHIP THICKEN

"Sara, it's time to get up. We should be at the Balsalms' in 15 minutes. Are you okay with that?"

Waking up out of a deep sleep was refreshing, momentarily. Then the reality of the recent strange development overtook the brief respite her nap had provided. Here it was only the second day, a little after noon to be exact, and already Sara's experiences had been both upbeat and unpleasant.

She and Gram touched briefly on what had transpired. Was this latest incident really about Sara, or was it related to her connection to the Ambassador? Should they distance themselves from the Balsalm family? Perhaps they could explain that they were uncomfortable with the situation, hoping their new friends would understand. Why did George Balsalm want to see them in his suite? These were all perplexing points to think about. They finally decided not to do or say anything until after the meeting with the Ambassador.

When they got to the Balsalms' suite, Linc opened the door to welcome them. As they walked in, their mouths dropped, figuratively. The word grandeur was not adequate enough to describe what was laid out before them. The penthouse suite was one of a kind. The huge living room was bordered on two sides by floor-to-ceiling windows with French doors leading out to a balcony the length of the room. Elegant tapestry couches and chairs in shades of blue, burgundy, and cream; ornately carved tables; and Oriental rugs gave the room an air of class and fine taste.

Within a few minutes, the rest of the family joined them in the living room. They greeted Sara and Gram warmly, making them feel comfortable and just like part of the family.

"Would you like to have a tour before we have lunch?" Anne offered. "Originally, as Pat knows, a few of us were just going to have salad; but now that everyone will be eating together, lunch will have more substance."

Both ideas sat well with Gram and Sara. Sara had been too tired to eat in their room, so by now she was famished. And after seeing the impressive living room, her curiosity about the rest of this palatial suite was certainly piqued.

The dining room was adjacent to the living room. The center of interest here was the huge table laden with much more than salad! From there, they moved into a galley kitchen, a long and narrow room with stainless steel appliances along one side and the sink and counter on the other side. Gleaming pans hung decoratively from a rod above the stove. A man wearing a white uniform and a chef's hat with the ship's emblem appeared to be in charge of lunch.

After walking through a formal-looking office with a mahogany desk and a built-in bookcase, they entered a wide hall leading to five bedrooms. One could only wonder what their home was like!

"Sara, you have to come see my room," insisted Martha, jumping up and down.

Hand in hand, the two walked to Martha's bedroom. It was a large, bright room with full-length windows.

"I didn't want her to have a balcony," Anne whispered to Sara, checking that Martha wasn't able to hear. "Too dangerous!"

Sara certainly agreed, picturing a five-year-old outside alone with only a railing to protect her.

Martha's bed was covered with special toys, such as cuddly teddy bears and a doll that obviously was a favorite, showing the scars of a well-loved friend. Sara bent over and whispered that this room was her favorite, which caused an immediate smile to join Martha's extraordinary eyes in lighting up the child's face.

"Let's eat!"

Whoever made that suggestion got a positive response. Eight companions quickly sat down to enjoy lunch. Anne kept the conversation upbeat and entertaining. When the meal was over, George asked Sara and Gram to join him in his office. Sara's trembling started again.

George explained that there was more to the story than just his being appointed ambassador to Italy, although that alone was a great honor. He could not fill them in on the details, as they were top secret. However, he did tell them that a high-ranking third-world official was seeking asylum at the Embassy. This man's country would stop at nothing to get hold of him before he could divulge information about their political corruption.

"Whoever tried to cause trouble for you probably thought you were someone else, possibly even connected to our family," George surmised. "Now that we know there is danger, security for us is on red alert until the problem is resolved. I am going to move into the Embassy by myself. People posing as the rest of my family will stay there with me. The plan is to fool the assailants into thinking that these decoys are my family until the situation is cleared.

"Anne, Leanne, Martha, Linc, and Martin will all stay at a villa in Rome. Here is what I would like to propose to you. It's something Anne and Leanne brought up right before you arrived. You mentioned earlier that you are planning to spend three nights in Rome, so they suggested, and I heartily concur, that you spend those three nights at our villa. No one knows about this villa except a handful of my top trusted people. You will have a chauffeured limousine at your disposal. If you want anyone from our family to join you on your excursions, that's fine. But it is completely up to you."

"Why do you want to do this?" Gram asked pointedly. "Even though we have become friends and thoroughly enjoy your company, we really don't know you that well."

"I understand your question, and it is right on the mark. The attempt on Sara would not have taken place if it were not for her connection with our family. The assailants have no knowledge that our friendship is so new. It would not be safe for you to stay in Italy as the situation stands. You do have the option of flying home, but the bottom line is that my family would love to have you as our guests."

Gram sat silent for several moments even though George had finished. Finally she replied, "George, this is a lot to take in. Sara and I certainly have to discuss it first. How about our family back home? What will we tell them? What about our hotel and those assigned to help us in Rome? We have so many questions and need time to explore the situation. May we have a few hours before answering you?"

"Of course, Pat. If you choose to stay at the villa, you'll be as safe as if you'd never met us since no one knows about the villa. I do have to caution you, though, that if you decide to stay there, your family can't know the details. Why don't we continue our discussion tonight after dinner?

"From now on, you will be observed at all times by one of our staff members. You won't even be aware of our security staff. Siobhan will still be on hand to help with your shipboard needs. Feel free to do whatever you want. If you wish to return home, we will make it possible for that option when we disembark."

With that, Gram and Sara said their goodbyes to the family. Martha wanted Linc and Sara to take her to the wave pool. She looked so disappointed when it didn't work out. Sara promised to sit next to her at dinner in the dining hall. Her sweet little face brightened up with that news.

It was time for Sara and Gram to come up with a "yes" or "no." It would require deep discussion—no doubt about that.

17 TO DO OR NOT TO DO

It was late afternoon when Sara and Gram returned to their room. Kicking off their shoes, they sat down on two comfortable chairs and looked at each other. Laughter permeated the air—yes, laughter—not just a trickle of laughter but hysterical laughter, laughter that causes tears to run down cheeks, noses to run, and choking sounds to escape from throats. You get the picture. They were laughing at something that had little humor. It cleared the air, though.

Gram's first audible words were "How did we get in this situation?"

"I haven't a clue."

"Sara, first of all, we don't have to go anywhere near that villa. We can just go home. I would be afraid to follow our original plans. If we," and she emphasized *we*, "decide to join them, there are issues to be settled. Exactly how do you feel? Either way is fine with me."

Sara knew everything Gram had said was absolutely true. If the problems on the ship hadn't happened, she would have voted for the villa hands down. Maybe because she was young, the previous encounter didn't seem so ominous to her now. But all the facts had to be reviewed.

The Balsalms were wonderful. They offered a chance to sample a lifestyle Sara might never be exposed to again. This 15-year-old was always up for a challenge. Pros and cons bounced back and forth. What would they tell their family? Was it really safe at the villa? Last but not least, were they sure this was what they wanted to do?

Finally, they came to a decision that pleased both of them. Yes, they wanted to go to the villa. If they were uneasy about anything once they got there, they would make plans to return home immediately. Their cell phones would be working again once they were on land, so they could communicate with everyone.

The story to the family would be absolutely true, since their emails had mentioned joining up with the Balsalms. Now the tale would refer to the villa invitation. The only thing they would leave out was the intrigue. They felt bad about that omission, but it had to be part of the decision.

"Let's wait until after we speak to George before we email the family," Gram suggested.

No problem with that. They dressed for new evening adventures and were off. Dinner in the dining hall went as if no one had a care in the world. They decided to have dessert in the Balsalm suite in an hour. Sara wanted to look in the shops for some gift ideas first.

18 IT'S A GO!

Martha answered the knock, jumping up and down while opening the door for Gram and Sara. She was like a yo-yo, full of joy. Linc was right in back of her. When Sara saw him, she gave him a thumbs up. His face lit up.

"Sara, do you like my dress?" the package of energy asked, holding the skirt of her powder blue dress with its crisp white pinafore slightly covering it and then gleefully twirling around so they could see the back as well.

"I love it. You remind me of Alice in Wonderland in your beautiful dress."

Sara knew somebody must have read *Alice in Wonderland* to her. That darling little lady loved being read to, even at the pool. There were books geared to her age all around their suite. (Sara used the word *suite* but what she really meant was *mansion.)*

"I love Alice! I love Alice!"

"Come into the dining room." A smiling Linc motioned as he invited them in.

It was amazing how a family as wealthy and worldly as they were also so down to earth. Even the way they all dressed was in good taste, never flashy—certainly not like families trying to impress. Sara loved the way Gram fit in.

People enjoyed her humor and warmhearted responses, as well as being so knowledgeable and, something Sara liked best, a good listener.

Sara felt quite presentable wearing a beige gold dress with a short skirt. She bought it for a school dance. At that time there were two options. One was simple, almost understated, and the other was a similar color but had layers of crisp material that made the skirt stick out. There was lots of bling on the top. Both were workable for the dance, but she had chosen the simpler dress. Did she pick the right one! Bling would not have worked tonight.

The table was spread with heavenly looking desserts and pitchers of alcoholic and non-alcoholic drinks. She spotted her favorite, iced tea, and had picked up a glass to pour herself some when a formally dressed bartender appeared to do the job. She hadn't even seen him. The others were already there, nibbling and filling the air with light conversation. Someone mentioned the evening show. Tonight a comedian was the entertainment. That was appealing.

At this point, George walked over to Gram and Sara, then pointed to the office. Once they were alone, Gram began the conversation. "Our decision is made, but we do have things to discuss."

She told him it would be a pleasure to join the family at the villa, but they had questions. The conversation went back and forth until Gram was satisfied that this was indeed the best choice for her and Sara. George was so happy about the decision.

George had already figured out a plan. He would contact the hotel people where Sara and Gram were slated to stay. Two people would register there, one older woman and one teenage girl who resembled Gram and Sara. The impostors would go in and out of the hotel a few times during the three days of their stay. After all, no one knew the real Dischinos. A separate car would take Gram and Sara to the villa.

Sara and Gram would stay at the villa. If at any time they felt uneasy, George would make arrangements for them to fly back to the USA. He approved of what they planned to tell their family about staying at the villa. There was no need to worry them unnecessarily.

After determining that they had covered everything, they returned to the dining room to finish their desserts, feeling they had made the right choice.

19 A KINDRED SPIRIT

Days three and four flew by with no unpleasant incidents. Sara and Katherine never ended up going to the disco night. On that day they ran into each other at the wave pool, the connection was immediate, and the two girls began to talk as if they had known each other for ages.

Katherine had a younger brother named Anthony, who was the same age as Sara's brother. Katherine spoke of her parents, including the fact that her mom was a lawyer and her dad was a doctor. They had such high expectations, which Katherine never felt she could meet. She also mentioned how her parents were often away due to their time-consuming occupations. Katherine was clearly upset about this.

The Nanny who had taken care of her since birth was still with her. This tiny Japanese-American lady played more than the role of a caregiver. She provided stability and love to Katherine. Katherine no longer called her "Nanny" but used the American version of her Japanese name. Through the years, Cheri had taken her charge to visit her parents, who lived in the Bronx. They were gentle, loving people. Katherine adored those visits.

After an hour sitting at the wave pool, the girls decided

to go shopping. What better way to bond than shop? The ship had a variety of stores. There was something for everybody. The stores displayed unique merchandise, tempting potential customers to spend. First they went to a high-end shoe store, where 20 pairs of heels left their boxes and adorned teenage feet. Sara amused herself by trying on a $300 pair of Jimmy Choo's on sale for $200. Katherine and she laughed at what the store considered a sale. Tired from shopping, the girls stopped at the Teen Lounge and ordered something cool to drink.

Katherine mentioned that she lived in Manhattan. Sara thought she had found a new friend. Wrong. She had found a kindred spirit! Sara had also lived in New York City for several years. This added another dimension to their already blossoming friendship.

She went on to ask Katherine a million questions about day-to-day life as a New Yorker. They discussed favorite "Big Apple" attractions, and both loved the Broadway theater.

Overall, it was a great day. Sara went back to the room and told Gram about her newly found friendship with Katherine. Gram was, of course, delighted to hear all of it! Sara said she planned to hang out with Linc the next day and maybe Katherine too!

20 A REALLY GOOD TIME

After a satisfying night of sleep, Sara hopped out of bed, got ready, and went down to the Teen Lounge to meet Linc. They had a buffet breakfast. Sara went for the French toast, and Linc went for cereal. He told Sara he would love French toast, but, unfortunately, he was allergic to eggs.

After breakfast, they ordered a few non-alcoholic drinks and played some video games in the arcade. Sara saw a photo booth and had to take some pictures with Linc so she'd remember this moment forever. Just in time, Sara saw Katherine at the Teen Lounge playing Pac-Man and dragged her into the photo booth. Sara, Linc, and Katherine must have spent a half hour in that photo booth, taking the wackiest pictures ever seen by man. It was all such a blast. Linc and Katherine seemed to be getting along so well, not that Sara feared they wouldn't. It was truly a whimsical day full of laughter and fun.

At the end of the day, Sara felt gratitude for meeting two people whom she truly liked.

21 HE ASKED ME!
HE REALLY ASKED ME!

On day five, an upbeat shipboard entertainment was a backstage tour that included meeting a Broadway cast. One of the cast members was rehearsing "Bring Him Home" from *Les Mis*.

Sara complemented him when he finished and related that she sang "Castle in the Clouds" for several different occasions, as well as auditions. They talked a bit more and then, to Sara's astonishment, he made an announcement to the whole tour group and the practicing cast.

"Hey, listen up, group. This young lady," pointing to Sara, "not only is familiar with *Les Mis* but sang 'Cosette's solo.' How about asking Sara to sing for us?"

"Please floor, open up and let me fall through," Sara wished silently.

She couldn't remember being so embarrassed. There was no turning back. She walked up to the piano accompanist, noting he was rifling through his music, searching for something suitable. They picked "How Lovely To Be a Woman" and "I Could Have Danced All Night." The man at the piano smiled, noting how appropriate the songs were considering the mixed age group.

The reception she received was fantastic. The tour group must have been in a benevolent mood and extremely kind, for Sara was met with rousing applause. Being the ham that she was, her embarrassment soon subsided and pleasure took over.

"I am only going to say three words: You were phenomenal!" Gram's face had a special glow of pride.

The two were on a "high" walking back to the cabin to check email before going to lunch. Once they got inside, they filled the room with the laughter and babbling that only true joy can cause.

Sara's email from her father was all positive. He said that since this opportunity doesn't happen to everyone she should enjoy every moment. Sara wondered how he would feel if he knew the whole story but mentally squelched that thought.

Mom sent a funny email containing a cartoon that cracked her up. It showed a girl who was far from home looking forlorn as she read her email. There was a cloud above her with the word "homesick" inserted. In the next frame the mother was sitting with a woman whose attaché case read "INTERIOR DESIGN." The third segment pictured a room all redone as an office with a caption, "We decided to make a few changes to your room. The chair pulls out to be a single bed. It is so comfortable." Her mom ended by including warm wishes of love.

AJ's message really got to her: "Sara, I don't know what a villa is. Please send me a picture. When are you coming home?"

AJ was telling her he missed her, even though he probably didn't realize it.

Sara realized that she missed her family. But that feeling quickly vanished with the ring of the telephone. Gram went to answer it, then turned it over to Sara with a shrug accompanied by a wide smile.

"Sara, this is Steven Wilson from the 'On Broadway' show. Thank you so much for the performance. You are really good. You've got talent, young lady."

Sara managed to mouth some sort of a thank you response. Her heart was doubling up on its beats.

"I have a favor to ask of you. One of our vocalists has a terrible sore throat and will not be able to perform. She has three numbers. Do you think you could stand in for her? Her voice range is quite similar to yours. Are you up to it?"

More mumbles, heart racing wildly, culminating with a definite "yes."

"Are you a member of Equity?"

Sara wasn't quite sure what "Equity" was, but certainly it wasn't anything she had ever joined and she told Steven that.

"Well, unfortunately, we can't pay you then, but we would like you to have dinner with us beforehand. They are also recording this show, and we'll be happy to give you a copy."

This was so exciting. There was no question of acceptance, which Sara gave for both dinner and the performance. She also asked Steven if her grandmother could join them.

"Of course! Now that that's settled, can you come around 2:00 for rehearsal? We meet right at the stage where you performed."

After thanking him again, Sara promised to be there promptly at 2:00.

Gram got on the house phone to the Balsalms and told them there was interesting news to share. Where were they going to be?

Anne mentioned they were staying in the room for lunch as Martha was so tired she had fallen asleep. "Come over and join us. I was about to call you."

That seemed to be a good idea, but first Sara wanted to send her news flying over cyberspace. Four emails sailed across the ocean to announce she would be onstage with a few qualifying details.

Sara's thoughts went to Katherine. They had planned to get together, and Sara was dying to tell her the news. The two had hit it off well together, so Sara thought Katherine wouldn't think she was bragging. She made a quick call to Katherine's room. It was her mother who answered. She told Sara that Katherine was at the pool but would be back shortly.

"Just tell Katherine to make sure she goes to the show tonight. Maybe I will get to see her before."

She only had an hour and a half before rehearsal and had to keep that in mind. They left for the Balsalms' suite to share Sara's opportunity to do a totally unexpected performance. Gram suggested maybe Linc could look for Katherine while Sara was practicing. That wasn't a bad idea.

The Balsalms were elated with the news and they showed it.

"I didn't know you were so talented. There's no question as to where we will be tonight," Linc's dad remarked.

Linc raised his fists and smiled broadly.

It was time to go. Gram and Linc accompanied Sara. Then Linc went to the pool to find Katherine. Before Gram left, she wanted to know what time rehearsal would be over. Sara was clueless.

"Well, page me on the walkie-talkie and I'll meet you right here. Get the info on where we will eat dinner. Good luck, Baby Girl."

Sara went into the theater feeling she was floating on air while inner butterflies formed a queasy stomach. The rehearsal went well. She had an assistant director who worked with her exclusively until she was ready to join the cast. Her songs were familiar, giving a boost to her confidence.

22 A HIGH NOTE

Eating dinner with the Broadway production group was utterly awesome. Gram and Sara were included in every aspect of a lively conversation. What an upbeat group! It would have been even better if dinner were after the show because the anticipation of performing kept Sara from relaxing and enjoying the banter of this talented group.

After her performance, Sara couldn't believe she had done it! She had actually performed with a professional group. The sound of applause while she was taking her bows told her the performance had gone well. "It's Not Easy Being Green," her first solo, brought loud applause. Sara realized it had been a good choice. Much of her audience was familiar with *Sesame Street* and enjoyed Kermit's soliloquy. Later she sang the selected songs "I Really Like New York," an old song by Kander and Ebb, and "This Is My Beloved," from the musical *Kismet*, with such animation that resounding applause resulted. Sara took her bows with the cast, feeling she had done her job well.

Congratulations, kudos, thumbs up bombarded the entertainer at the program's completion. The Balsalms, Katherine, and Gram were especially vocal in their praise.

Leanne asked them back to their suite to celebrate. She also extended the invitation to Katherine, who was thrilled, having heard a description of the penthouse digs. Even though Sara was exhausted, this was not to be missed.

She went back to thank the theater crew. They hugged her, saying soon her name would be in lights. Then she went to the Balsalms' suite to join her friends.

The dining room table was laden with yummies. Katherine was in awe of this display, as well as the Balsalms' living quarters.

"What kind of job do these people have?" Katherine whispered.

"Something in the government, but I think the family has always been wealthy."

"Wow!"

Linc walked over to remark how impressed he was with her voice. Then he kidded about her lack of talent at the climbing wall. She still hadn't made it to the top.

Since tomorrow was the last full day onboard ship, Katherine, Linc, and Sara decided to have breakfast together at the Windstream, a more casual place. The euphoria held as the hour grew late. Promising to meet tomorrow and thanking their hosts repeatedly, Gram and Sara separated from the group. What an evening it had been!

23 EUPHORIA TAKES A DIVE

Sara flopped onto the bed to let the evening sink in. After a few minutes, she groggily arose to get ready for bed. When she opened the chest drawer to get her pajamas, something struck her as not right. Normally, she placed her clothes in their proper drawer, but that's all. This drawer's garments were neatly folded. Was it the room attendant who did this or Gram? Gram was in the bathroom, getting ready for bed. While she waited for her to come out, Sara went to the closet to get her robe. Her clothes were not in the same order. The bathing suit cover-up she had worn earlier in the day was hung up over a dress. That had not been her doing.

When Gram came out of the bathroom, Sara brought her up to date. The euphoria had vanished and distress took over.

"Sara, check your bag!"

Her bag had never left the room at all. It contained all her vital information, passport, cell phone, etc. She had carried around a small backpack with her shipboard card and a few other things during the day. When dress was more formal, she used a tiny gold purse to carry bare essentials. She kept the bag in the bottom drawer of her chest. A better spot would have been the safe. Checking out its contents, Sara noticed once again that something was not right. Her passport should have been in one of the zippered pockets. It was in the bag—but in a different place.

"Is anything missing, Sara?"

"I don't think so, but things have been moved."

"Are you sure nothing is missing?"

Upon examining the bag again, Sara discovered one thing was missing. "The letter that had our itinerary on it is gone. It has the name of our hotels and the people we are to meet. You have the same letter. See if yours is missing."

Gram found her letter in her folder with all the information, but the pleasure that they had when they entered the room was gone. A feeling that they had been violated, combined with being at a loss about what to do, caused deep uncertainty. They realized Siobhan wouldn't be able to help them with this. After a few minutes of back-and-forth conversation, they made a clear-cut decision. George Balsam should be contacted right then and there.

"Remember, Sara, we have the option of not going to the villa," Gram offered while dialing the Balsalms' suite.

The Ambassador came right to their room. While he listened intently, his face took on a frown of serious concern. "Well," he concluded, "your privacy has been breached—unforgivable! There is one good outcome, though. Whoever did this has your original itinerary, so the villa really seems the place to be now."

They hadn't thought about that. George proposed they go right along with the plan. It seemed logical, and they knew they could always get a plane and return home if they felt unsafe. George left, assuring them of complete safety. Although they still had an uneasy feeling, both of them were so tired that sleep came easily.

24 ANOTHER PREDICAMENT

A good night's rest made everything look more acceptable. This was day six. One more day and they would be away from whomever was spying. Sara's plan was to avoid being alone. Gram accompanied her for breakfast at sea, deciding to enjoy friends and shipboard offerings.

After breakfast Gram went to see George to review plans. Then sunbathing was on the agenda. A relaxing time would prepare them for the next segment of their trip. Sara would join up with Linc and Katherine. Being watched didn't spoil the enjoyment of sharing a perfect day. If anything, it invoked a sense of security. Gram paged Sara frequently. All exchanged enjoyable moments. Leanne brought Martha to share the last swim. Katherine and Sara exchanged cell phone numbers plus other essentials needed for future communications.

The day went quickly. Soon it was late afternoon and packing became a priority. It would take at least two hours to pack and get ready for the dressy farewell dinner. Disembarking was early the next morning, and this special time was coming to an end.

As Sara and Linc walked together toward the elevators, he asked, "Do you know what the show is going to be tonight?"

"I think it's going to be that great comedian, along with a few vocalists. I don't know if I want to go. I'm sure it will be good, but I'm tired," she responded.

Sara was also thinking about how complex tomorrow was sure to be, an even more trying thought.

"Look spiffy for dinner, Linc."

They separated by the elevator. Sara forgot to call Gram before Linc left. She took the elevator to her deck and pulled the door handle to enter the hall leading to the cabin. It was locked. That wasn't good. Sara scolded herself for not contacting Gram. Where were the people who were supposed to be "watching" her? She tried paging Gram on the walkie-talkie. Dead silence!

Another entrance to the room came to mind, but it was necessary to go back up the stairs and go forward toward the front of the ship. Rushing along, her heart kept beating double time! She finally reached the stairs and took them two at a time. At the top there were cones blocking the down side of the alternating stairs, with a handwritten sign stating repairs were being made. Luckily, the elevator was close by. No one else was around as Sara stepped in and pushed the correct button. The door closed, but nothing happened. She pushed the button to reopen it, but that didn't work either.

Next she tried the walkie-talkie, with no response. Checking the batteries proved that was the problem. There were no batteries. Someone had removed them. She remembered leaving the walkie-talkie on her chair while Linc, Katherine, and she were playing in the pool with Martha. That was when the batteries were probably taken.

She banged on the elevator door over and over again. Then to add to her dread, the lights went out.

It seemed like forever before a voice responded to her battering. "Hold on. I'll get you out."

What beautiful words. A lot of discussion took place, but no action. Something was happening. Part of the ceiling of the elevator opened. The man who found a way to save the frightened girl was no other than Simon. Was he a hero or the pursuer?

"I happened to be walking by the elevator when I heard your banging. I knew they were repairing the doors but didn't know both doors to your deck were locked. Are you all right?"

She answered that she was fine but frightened. It was strange that no one was around. This had not happened to anyone else. She dismissed the incident as unfortunate but not malicious, not wanting to let fear be invasive.

"I'm glad you were near to hear me. It wasn't fun being stuck in a pitch-black elevator. I've got to get to my room. Gram will be worried. Thank you, Simon."

"Take care, Sara. Enjoy the rest of your vacation. Where are you staying in Rome?"

She remembered George Balsalm's directions not to tell anyone about the villa. The original hotel was the name she gave Simon.

"Oh, you'll like the hotel. It's in a great location. Let's see if they are finished repairing the door."

The cones were gone and the door opened easily. Simon went on his way, and Sara hurried to the room. Gram looked relieved to see her.

"I was so worried when you didn't answer your 'walkie.' Then I realized you couldn't answer, as your 'walkie' had no batteries."

"How did you know that, Gram?"

She explained that a ship's attendant had knocked on the door of the room and handed her the batteries. "He said a young lady named Katherine had found them by the pool and thought they belonged to you. I knew the walkie-talkie was useless without them."

The explanation seemed logical, although there were some flaws. If the batteries had fallen out, why was the battery compartment on the "walkie" closed? She certainly would have noticed the battery door. It seemed to be a minor point and really unimportant. Later, she would realize that she should have given more thought to this detail. Simon's elevator appearance was more than a coincidence. However, she didn't know that at the time.

Sara didn't tell Gram about the elevator. She thought it would upset her.

Unfortunate choice, Sara!

25 NOT QUITE THE YELLOW BRICK ROAD

That evening everyone assembled for cocktails back at the Outrigger Salon. They had been together for six days, but these new acquaintances were "keeper" friends. At dinner, they shared special remembrances to reflect upon when they traveled different paths. The entire group attended the show, which was quite enjoyable. All too soon, the cruise would be a part of their past.

At the end of the evening, George Balsalm presented Gram with a wrapped package, mentioning it was a *Fodor's Essential Italy* travel guide. "This is the best guide for a short-term stay. It highlights the 'must sees.'" Given in a much lower voice, his instructions were to read it carefully, emphasizing the word *carefully*.

At this point, a big show was made of saying goodbyes, and then everyone went back to their rooms to finish last-minute details.

Gram opened the *Fodor's* not knowing what to expect. While looking through the book, she discovered George's directions pasted over the original page 30.

"Sara, listen to this. George left us instructions on what

to do tomorrow: Go through customs; then follow signs to the luggage pickup. Look for 'la toilette' sign. You will find it as soon as you leave customs and arrive in the promenade. It is located between a McDonald's and a large newsstand. In front of the 'la toilette' will be a woman with white hair around Pat's age, dressed in white slacks and a multi-colored, short-sleeved blouse. Ask her for the directions to the luggage pickup. Tell her you like her blouse. She will give you instructions."

They looked at each other with the same expression and the same question in mind: were they doing the right thing?

"Come on, Gram. We're up to this adventure."

Their sleep that night consisted of tossing and turning.

26 SUBTERFUGE BEGINS

A knock at the door indicated that Room Service was delivering their breakfast. After they finished eating, they left the room and followed the ship's instructions on disembarking. Luggage was not a problem as it had been picked up the previous evening and would be ready for them to pick up once they were off the ship.

Going down the gangplank, they caught a glimpse of Simon way ahead of them and Sara waved. Her attitude toward him had changed somewhat since their first meeting. After all, he rescued her twice. Hero or not, Sara still wasn't sure. He would soon be past tense. They didn't see any of their friends on the way to the bus that took them to customs. Getting through customs was fairly easy, and they easily spotted the right "toilette."

True to George's directions, the woman he had described was standing in front of the door. After a brief discussion, this woman motioned them to follow her to a door close by. It had no title. She opened it with a key. Inside was a long hall with a number of doors along the way. Opening another door, the lady signaled them to enter. To their surprise, a girl Sara's age stood up from a bench.

The woman began her directives. She was wearing a pair of white slacks and a patterned blouse. The four were to switch clothes. There was even a baseball cap for Sara that covered much of her hair. This was really getting whacked. The clothes fit. How they knew sizes was a mystery. The feeling of not being in control and vulnerable added to their anxiety.

According to the powers that be, they were not to worry about luggage. It was already on its journey to the villa. There would be a man holding a sign saying "Bernardo" standing by the taxi exit. He was the limousine driver who would transport them to the villa. With no more instructions, the two left in their new clothes. Within ten minutes, the mission of finding "Bernardo" was complete. The limousine was the magic carpet to the next encounter.

Gram and Sara had no idea how long the trip would take, where the villa was located, or even its name. However, something wonderful had happened. They could use their cell phones that were specially programmed for foreign use. It was six hours earlier in New Jersey; so while Italian time was 11:00 a.m., it was only 5:00 a.m. at home. Sara called her parents. It was so good to hear their voices. A rapid-fire conversation exchange took place. Much of the voyagers' news had already been communicated through the technology of emails; however, Sara's parents knew nothing about the intrigue.

Mom told Sara that Grandpa was getting better every day. He had the best care from his daughter, Kim; and Sara's Uncle Kirk visited him daily.

After she talked to her Mom and Dad, AJ grabbed the phone and spoke nonstop, asking question upon question. He wanted to know the time in Italy, what the spaghetti was like, and when they were coming home. He ended by reminding Sara not to forget his present.

When the conversation was over, everyone's spirits were lifted. Sara and Gram agreed to do everything they could to enjoy the next three days.

Their expectation that the drive would be fairly long proved totally wrong. The signs kept pointing to Rome, while the mileage numbers diminished. In less than an hour they were in the city of Rome.

27 THEY MADE IT!

It wasn't long before the limousine parked in front of a humongous building. It looked as if it were built hundreds of years ago but was magnificently maintained. A large iron wall with a beautifully scrolled gate was obviously the entrance. The driver spoke on his cell phone, apparently to someone inside. He pulled away from his parking spot, turned right and then right again. At the second right, a sign appeared announcing this was the historical section of Rome. The Colosseum was right in view. Unbelievable! They were now in back of a mansion; this was no villa!

An iron gate, similar to the one in front of the building, opened. The limo wound its way up the driveway to the rear of the house. Of course, the first to greet them was Martha, smiling with pure pleasure. As Sara stepped out of the car, her arm was grabbed by this twirling bit of spontaneity.

Bouncing as always, she greeted the guests. "Sara, I'm so happy you're here. Wait till you see my room. Wait till you see the pool. It's fun here. Hi, Gram Pat."

Leanne and Linc were close behind Martha. "Well, I guess you have been duly welcomed. We truly are happy you are here. Come in and get yourselves settled," Leanne remarked as she gave each of them a warm welcoming hug.

Linc had a big welcome grin and shook both their hands. A teenage boy shaking hands with a teenage girl—that was one for the books! They followed the family as Martha held her grip on Sara. The back entrance led to a huge room that probably was the main entrance to the house. There were several different groupings of furniture, with chairs, sofas, and tables filled with antiques of every description and from various eras. One thing they all had in common was they were old and valuable.

"You made it. That's wonderful!" The welcoming voice came from behind them.

They turned around to see Anne opening the scrolled elevator copper grill gate. After a few minutes of pleasantries, Anne suggested everyone sit down. More conversation followed, during which Gram and Sara learned all about the area. The house was in a most central location, allowing them to see many sights by just walking; but a car would be available when needed. Is that class or what?

Leanne suggested that since they were here for only three days, a car tour might suite them. "We could all do that, if you'd like."

Her suggestion appealed to everyone.

"Let's have lunch first and then leave around 2:00. That gives you an hour to get settled. I know it's rushing you, but you only have three days."

A young girl Sara assumed was a maid introduced herself as Nina and then offered to lead them to their room, which looked like something out of a mansion. Two double beds with matching sapphire-blue satin bedspreads and draperies gave the room a regal look. One wall was graced by a large scrollwork mirror and another wall displayed an oil painting of a woman dressed in 19th-century garb and carrying a parasol. A tall chest of drawers, ornately decorated chairs, and a small round table completed the sumptuous furnishings. The bathroom and closets went along with the totally luxurious decor.

Sara and Gram quickly showered and changed, anxious to discover Rome.

A large van arrived for them after lunch. The "Eternal City" was about to be exposed. Martha made sure her seat was right next to Sara's, and she was bubbling with conversation as the top Roman sights unfolded before them. It was like opening a 3D history book as the Colosseum, Roman Forum, St Peter's Basilica, Vatican, Trevi Fountain, The Pantheon, Spanish Steps, Castel Sant'Angelo, and Piazza Navona filled the pages. You name it. The driver pointed at and described it all.

The van made several stops, and Sara was thrilled that she actually got to throw coins in Trevi Fountain. Linc, standing a few feet away from Sara and enjoying the moment, turned slightly to take in the whole scene. As he did so, a cold chill enveloped his entire body. What he saw were two dark-haired, mustached men staring intently at Sara. There was another man partially hidden but obviously with them. When they realized Linc had seen them, they immediately turned and disappeared into the crowd. Linc thought that the hidden man was Simon Kellar but couldn't be sure. The whole incident was so fleeting, almost too fast to comprehend.

Linc was confronted with a painful dilemma. If he told Sara what he had just seen, she would be on the next plane. He didn't want that. He chose to keep what had just happened to himself. This was a foolish mistake that would later have serious consequences. If he had given it careful consideration, he would have realized how dangerous it was for Simon to know their location. The secret wasn't secret anymore and was now capable of causing great pain.

After three hours, the tour was completed and the driver dropped the group at home. They were totally exhausted but impressed by all that Rome had to offer.

Martha was sound asleep, done in by the tour, so Linc and Sara thought the pool would be a relaxing option. The warm sun and the perfect temperature of the water created a delightful comfort zone.

As they sat on chairs by the pool, Linc swore Sara to secrecy before he began to unfold the happenings at the Embassy. Sara let him know she was a veritable vault at keeping secrets. They had a short time before they had to get ready for dinner, so Linc began his story in earnest.

28 TO SPEAK OR NOT TO SPEAK

"When we arrived here at the villa, we came in through the back entrance, just as you did. Then we walked into the huge room in the front and found three men waiting there to speak to Grandfather. One of them had a briefcase secured with a chain. Grandfather was upset because no one was supposed to know his family's location.

"I guess Grandfather felt they should have their discussion in a more secluded spot. He led the intruders to a nearby room and then closed the door, ensuring the conversation would be private. The rest of my family followed a maid to get settled in their rooms. I decided to wait for you and your grandmother to arrive.

"Walking farther down the hall in the direction in which the men had gone, I noticed another door on the same side. When I opened it, I discovered a huge theater with a closed gold curtain made of a heavy brocade material.

"Trying not to make a sound, I tiptoed up the stage stairs and pulled back the curtain slightly. I heard voices coming from a room adjacent to the back of the stage but only recognized Grandfather's voice. The door in that room was ajar, and it was all that separated me from them.

I don't even think the people inside noticed the door."

Linc kept looking around to make sure that no one was within hearing range. He continued in such a low voice that Sara had to ask him to repeat some information several times.

"I sat by the wall near the door, twisting at times to peer into the room, trying to match faces with voices. Every word came through as if I were sitting in that room. The man who had been carrying the chain-wrapped briefcase did most of the talking. He told Grandfather that the refugee was a senior member of a Middle Eastern country's government. He was requesting asylum because his government had been infiltrated by a terrorist group capable of doing political harm to his homeland. While he was seeking asylum, his plan was exposed by the terrorists. Now there was a price on his head. The word was that his oppressors would do anything to keep him from divulging classified secrets, including kidnapping a few high-level Embassy people. Such a move would give the terrorist group a huge leverage. One of the other men quickly assured Grandfather that no one knew the location of his family, so they would be safe."

Linc considered telling Sara about the incident at the Trevi Fountain but decided against it. Instead, he once again pleaded with Sara to keep everything he was telling her secret. His grandfather would be extremely upset if he knew that Linc had been eavesdropping.

This really put Sara in in the middle of a horrible dilemma. If she told her grandmother what Linc had overheard, which Sara felt obligated to do, they would be on a plane out of Rome before the day was over. The cat would be out of the bag, and Linc would be in terrible trouble with his family! For all she knew, the United States government could be in trouble. All these things were significant concerns.

Linc was quite likable, not as a boyfriend but as a good friend. And loyalty was important to Sara. But a disturbing gut feeling was telling her that this might be a regrettably wrong decision. After a few moments' consideration, Sara decided to keep quiet anyway. (A little advice to anyone facing an unpleasant quandary: go with your gut feeling!)

With a lump in the pit of her stomach, Sara left the pool to get ready for dinner. Two more full days and nights here and then she and Gram would leave for Gaeta. Once they were there, this burden would disappear, and she would feel so relieved. However, she appreciated these awesome people who had been so kind, and visiting Rome was without precedent. This truly was a complex situation.

It had been one week since Sara had left home. She couldn't believe all that had happened. It was enough to fill a book.

Dinner was an epicurean delight, but enjoying it proved to be a struggle. All Sara could think of was Linc's hush hush message. At last it was time to go to bed. In their room, Gram was full of her usual humor as she described an amusing incident with Martha. The youngster wanted to go into the pool, but no one could find her bathing suit. Finally, Leanne discovered she had it on under her clothes. She had put it on earlier and forgotten all about it. Her answer to this discovery set them all laughing—"I must be losing my mind!"

This was a common expression her grandmother often used, but it seemed so surprising to hear it from the mouth of this little munchkin. Sara laughed but at the same time could have cried for her deception of the grandmother she loved.

The next two days were spent seeing more of what this seven hill city of Rome had to offer. It's amazing how much you can explore when transportation is taken care of by a chauffeured van. Sara and Gram shared these enlightening journeys with the Balsalms while the Ambassador struggled with the conflict at the Embassy.

29 NO LONGER A HERO

The last day with Linc and his family began with mixed emotions. Being with the Ambassador's family was a momentous experience; however, the anxiety Sara encountered was overwhelming. Her deception wasn't helping. Hiding a secret like this was difficult.

At breakfast, the conversation centered around what sight to visit. Anne and Leanne suggested Via Montone and Castel Romano, which were high-fashion districts.

Gram responded enthusiastically to that game plan. "I would love the opportunity to see those gorgeous creations. I do want to be with Sara, so whatever she wants to do is fine with me."

To reassure Gram, Anne interjected that George had repeatedly recounted the fact that they were all being protectively followed. Sara would have gladly joined the fashion expedition, but that would have left Linc without a buddy.

"Linc, you mentioned the Colosseum. We never did get to tour that. Why don't we go there? It's so close," Sara suggested.

She could see Linc's eyes light up as she proposed this alternative, guessing he had been picturing a day alone. No way would he join a shopping tour. Gram's reluctance to be away from Sara was obvious, but Anne's comment about protection somewhat alleviated her concern. The final decision was that the ladies would shop, Linc and Sara would tour the Colosseum, and Martha would stay at the house with one of the servants she really liked.

Before leaving, Sara went out to the back courtyard to take pictures of the beautiful villa. Martha begged to join. Sara saw no reason not to take her, and Leanne agreed. Camera in hand, with Martha bouncing while holding tightly to her arm, she left the house.

She took several pictures of the house, with Martha taking center stage. What a ham Miss Mary Jane Shoes was! Taking a photo so the entire house would be in the picture proved difficult. The wall surrounding the house cropped a full view, so Sara searched for a better location. She noticed a small door in the wall that hadn't been obvious before. She unlocked it and peered outside. If she crossed the street, most of the house would be visible.

Instructing Martha to remain inside the wall, Sara began to cross the street. She noticed a group of four or five men huddled closely together, obviously in deep conversation and so involved that they didn't notice her crossing.

Then she realized that one of the men was Simon! Her first thought was to call out to him. After all, he was her hero after rescuing her from that scary situation in the ship's elevator. But that idea faded quickly when she considered the present scene.

Why was Simon here, and why was he with those other men? She quickly finished crossing the street and moved behind a large, dense bush where she could observe Simon while she was well hidden. She just hoped Martha wouldn't come out of that small door looking for her.

Afraid to cross the street back to the house until they left, she waited until the group began to disband. One man stayed, moving to one side of a tree in order to conceal his presence from the house.

She didn't know how to cross the street without being seen. Luckily, he left his spot and started walking in the opposite direction. His back was toward her as she dashed across the street and into the courtyard. Martha was a little upset at being left alone so long, but she perked up when Sara reappeared.

Now Sara faced another predicament. She didn't know if she should tell anyone about what had just happened. The entire situation was intolerable. This was her first experience having to make such crucial decisions. She wanted Gram's advice. She wanted her parents' advice. She'd even welcome advice from her brother, AJ. For a little kid, he was pretty smart.

She finally decided that the only one to confide in was Linc. When she told him what had just happened, he was alarmed but still swore Sara to secrecy. She was now coming to the conclusion that Linc was not thinking clearly. Fear had taken over logic. At this point, she wanted to tell all, but loyalty to Linc won out. Not a wise decision, Sara!

30 THE WEB OF FEAR IS SPUN

Later that morning, Linc and Sara found themselves walking along the Piazza del Colosseo to the Colosseum, which was only a few blocks away from the villa. She was a nervous wreck, expecting to be kidnapped at any moment.

After purchasing tickets for the next tour in English, they sat down to wait. Linc, always hungry, bought two gelatos from a nearby vendor.

As they entered this gigantic ancient ruin, her concerns melted away. The tour was fabulous. A guide told stories that amazed them. They listened with utter fascination. The part where the gladiators fought to their deaths one after another chilled them to the bone, especially when the guide noted that if too much blood was spilled, sawdust would be spread over it so the fights could continue. Sara thought she was pretty cool with scary stories. The movie *Misery* was a favorite, but this blew her mind. After the tour was over, she and Linc rattled on about the grisly details.

The Colosseum has many passages called *vomitoriums*, one of which they decided to explore before leaving. They used their imagination, along with the recent information they'd been given, to concoct some crazy contrived situations, which made them erupt into hysterical laughter.

As they prepared to leave, they became confused as to directions. "Let's go back the way we came in," Sara suggested.

As they reversed their direction, Sara suddenly froze. A short distance in front of them was a man she had seen before. She didn't know exactly where, though, since he disappeared into one of the many passages before she could get a better grasp on his identity. Linc, who had never seen the man, had no idea what was wrong. It took her a minute before she could tell him what she had just seen.

At this point, Sara guessed Linc was thinking she was overreacting. "Sara, I didn't see anything unusual. Maybe you're just on edge and that makes everyone look threatening."

With that statement Sara realized that Linc was so into keeping a lid on everything that he didn't want to hear what she had to say. Suddenly, she just wanted to get back to the villa and wait for tomorrow morning, when this dark scene would no longer be a problem.

"Maybe you're right," Sara said unconvincingly, wanting to stop a conversation that was going nowhere.

Something else was bothering her, but it was a fuzzy memory that floated in brief snatches. She couldn't bring it into focus.

"You know, Sara, we are supposed to be followed by Embassy people. Maybe that's who you saw."

That was a thought, although Sara was skeptical. She just didn't want to think about it anymore.

Back in her room, her mental fog lifted while she was getting ready for dinner. She had seen the mustached, dark-haired man in the Colosseum before—twice before. On the cruise, he was the man at the bottom of the stairs before Simon rescued her. He was also one of the men with Simon when she was taking pictures of the villa. Sara was unaware that he was also one of the men observing her at Trevi Fountain.

An unsettling chill forced Sara to decide this could not
go on. She kept repeating in her mind the cliché that Gram
often repeated, "You're dammed if you do and you're
dammed if you don't."

Was that ever the truth! The Balsams were the dearest
family. They hadn't seen George more than a few times
since their arrival because he was needed at the Embassy,
but Anne reported to them often. Sara could just imagine
the diplomatic intrigue that must be unfolding there!
Martin and Leanne were the most down-to-earth couple
imaginable.

Here was a family loaded to the hilt, able to buy all the
niceties of life, yet the kind of people you would choose to
have as lifetime friends. Martha, at five years old, was
completely unspoiled. Good manners complemented her
outgoing, loving personality. She was such a joy. Because
of her upbeat way, she was included in most activities.
Linc, now a close friend, did not have one unpleasant trait.
He never bragged or acted sarcastically, although he was
smarter and more worldly than any boy his age that she
knew. He wasn't much to look at, being short and thin.
She used the word "nerd" to describe him earlier. Now she
would take a nerd any time.

George joined them halfway through dinner. He
wanted to wish Sara and Gram goodbye, noting they were
"forever friends." Sara determined her next move. It's
amazing how making a decision brings relief!

Dinner was over, and an opportunity opened up.
George and Sara were the last to leave the dining room as
everyone went to another room for conversation and
relaxation. As soon as the others were out of sight, she
tapped George's shoulder and in a low voice asked if they
could meet secretly as a terrible situation had arisen.

"Sara, let's join the others right now. I will look for an
opportunity for a private conversation, but I suggest we
include your grandmother."

She hadn't thought about that. That would solve another problem, namely her guilt over keeping Gram in the dark. Sara still needed to let Linc know her plan of action, though.

31 UNRAVELING THE WEB

Decisions were now so much easier to make. They might not improve the Embassy's dilemma, but she knew she was doing the right thing. She walked over to where Linc was sitting on a love seat. There was just room enough for two. Perfect! He was reading *Fodor's* book on Rome, probably planning what to do tomorrow. She'd been talking with him for a few minutes when he mentioned that he wasn't feeling well. The whole situation was loathsome, and his stomach was reacting.

"Linc, I'm afraid what I am about to tell you will not improve your condition. I'm going to tell your grandfather what you overheard, plus all the bizarre events that have happened to me. Gram is going to be with me, although she knows nothing about a lot of it."

To her surprise, a look of relief passed over Linc's face. "Sara, this is the worst thing that has ever happened to me. But you're right. It's wrong to keep this all a secret. No matter what happens to me, I have to own up to my involvement. I didn't tell you this when you described the men you saw while you were taking pictures, but I think I saw two of them watching us when we were throwing coins in Trevi Fountain. Possibly one of them was the man we saw today at the Colosseum. I didn't tell you because I thought you would tell everything right then and there. I've been such a coward."

"Don't worry about that. I should have been open about all this craziness. Let's join the others."

Ambassador Balsalm joined Linc, Sara, Gram, and Anne in a game of 99, a card game Gram had taught Linc, Anne, and Leanne the first evening at the villa. Linc and Sara acted as if the roof were not about to cave in and kept the conversation humorous.

When the game was over, Ambassador Balsalm spoke loud enough for everyone to hear. "The time has come when our new and permanent friends will be leaving for their next adventure.

"Our families will certainly get together in the United States. I am looking forward to meeting Joe, Sara's parents, and AJ. I feel I know them already. Anne and I are returning to Connecticut for the Thanksgiving and Christmas holidays. We will definitely join up then, and we are inviting you to be our guests to celebrate."

Sara genuinely hoped his predictions would come true. Linc's and her house of cards could destroy that.

"I would like to offer a celebration drink for our friendship and a bon voyage. I had my secretary gather information about Gaeta for you two," he said, looking at Gram and then over to Sara. "Come into my office and I'll go over it with you."

Linc hopped up and asked if he could join them. George looked puzzled and Sara thought he was about to discourage him, so she blurted out that she would like that, nodding her head. He quickly got the message.

"I want to come too," Martha pleaded.

Even though Leanne was not in on the purpose of the meeting, she reminded Martha that it was bedtime. However, she told her that when she was ready for bed she could come down to say good night and goodbye. And with that, the bundle of energy dashed upstairs.

32 WHAT PATH TO TAKE

George led Sara and Gram into the same room where Linc had secretively listened to a conversation not meant for his ears. The Ambassador asked how they should begin. Sara began by letting Gram know the real purpose of this meeting and how sorry she was. Gram should have been let in on what was happening from the get go.

Noting Gram's bewildered look, Sara began to speak with a shaky voice. "It's hard to know where to begin. Maybe it should begin with Simon. Now that I think of it, Simon was always around when bad things happened. He was there to help by the steps when I was approached by that strange man and when I got stuck in the elevator. I didn't know if Simon was a hero or a villain. Then more bizarre things kept happening to me. Here's a good example: It was obvious someone had gone through my clothing in my dresser and closet. My itinerary for the entire vacation was missing. But you knew about all that."

The Ambassador nodded and asked her to continue. There were other incidents that Sara listed and described at length, including seeing Simon talking to three other men outside the villa, one of whom Sara thought was the man who blocked her path on the ship. Lastly, she related that at the Colosseum she caught sight of one of the men. Just recently, she realized that all these men had been on the cruise.

Next, Linc walked over to his grandfather and began his confession. "Grandpa, I know you will be disappointed with me. I'm so sorry I didn't tell you what I overheard when it happened."

Linc explained how and what he learned eavesdropping behind the stage. In addition, he admitted that he was guilty of keeping quiet and not supporting Sara when she wanted to tell all. And he finally told everyone about the Trevi Fountain incident.

Sara's expression of surprise and disappointment filled Linc with total remorse.

Gram's expression was a combination of bewilderment and alarm. "We went through all that trouble changing clothes with that woman and the child to avoid trouble for nothing. Sara, maybe we should skip Gaeta and go home. This is a bit too much intrigue for us," Gram declared in a none-too-steady voice.

Sara could see Gram was trying to be polite. She felt so guilty not having clued her in earlier. Whatever Gram wanted to do was fine. Not only had Gram been clueless, but no one at home had any idea of their undercover adventures in the first place. From the emails, the people at home thought they were in paradise. Well, to be truthful, it was paradise, with strings attached.

"Pat," George responded, "I know exactly how you feel, but I do have a plan that might help you feel more comfortable. I know how much you wanted to show Sara Gaeta, the place where her great grandparents lived. But first, let's put all this data together. I think we were all trying to spare each other worry but as a result muddied the waters unintentionally.

"I remember the incident before our first dinner at the Captain's table when that man introduced himself as Simon. He said he was a member of the Embassy 'attaché.'

As you know, I wasn't traveling as Ambassador but as a member of the 'attaché.' However, it did strike me as odd that he didn't know I was the Ambassador. I was not about to have anything to do with him at that point.

"I was mentally so involved with a serious problem at the Embassy that I gave him little thought. Now, in hindsight, I see that was a mistake. The only other time I saw the 'Cruise Simon' was when you had that incident in the stairwell. Come to think of it, I haven't run into Simon at the Embassy yet, which seems strange because I think I've met most of the staff by now. I'll have Security look into whether or not there really is a Simon Kellar on staff."

Turning to Linc, he said, "I'm sorry you didn't feel comfortable telling me what was going on before it came to this. I always thought you knew you could confide in me."

"I'm so sorry, Grandfather. And I apologize to Sara and her grandmother too." Linc's body language expressed much more than the few words he was able to utter.

With that, the Ambassador, Sara, Linc, and Gram returned to the dining room, where Martha, all ready for bed, was enjoying a biscotti while waiting to say goodbye.

She hugged her new friends with a touch of sadness. "Bye, Sara, I will miss you. You too, Gram."

Her mom gently escorted the little one to her room, reminding her to brush her teeth. When she returned, she said, "I don't know the whole story, but I know enough to realize you two have been through so many appalling issues, all because of your association with us. We feel terrible. You two are wonderful; and, Sara, you certainly didn't deserve any of this."

Anne concurred and spoke of future visits, when all this would be in the past. She also mentioned that this was a serious international situation and wished it would quickly be settled.

Gram assured them as best as she could that the Balsalms were not at fault and both she and Sara had nothing but the most affectionate feelings for them.

After remarking that the best of friendships can be formed under the oddest of circumstances, George went on to describe his solution. "I have a plan that will allow you to finish your trip with the utmost safety. Wear the same clothes you wore to come to this villa. A driver will take you to the airport and drop you off. A staff member of mine named Ted will be dressed in a red cap uniform. He will introduce himself to you, carry your luggage, and lead you to security. If anyone is trailing you, they will think you are taking the plane to the US.

Ted will meet you again after you go through customs and take you to a private jet that will fly you to Gaeta. When you land, a taxi driven by one of our people will deliver you to a different hotel than the one where you were originally registered to stay. You will be able to do everything you planned to do in Gaeta. When your visit there is over, one of our drivers will pick you up and drive you to the airport in Rome for your original flight home. Does that seem workable to you?"

It took Gram and Sara a few minutes to digest all this. Gram's first response to this offer was "George, this is completely unnecessary. You have done more for us than anyone could imagine."

The Ambassador broke in, quickly emphasizing his fondness for them. "Pat, don't feel that way. The situation is all on our side. We would feel so relieved if you would let us do this."

Gram quizzically looked at Sara to determine her reaction. "Be honest, Sara. I want you to answer exactly the way you feel."

This was really strange. An hour ago, Sara longed to be home, hugging the life out of her family. Now, after hearing the plan, she looked forward to completing their Italian odyssey. Her love of adventure won out every time. "I'm up for it if you are," she replied.

33 GAETA OR BUST

After breakfast and more farewells, Gram and Sara got into an official limo, luggage and all, and were driven to the airport. Final farewells took place in the courtyard. Their voices were not subtle in the least. Sara's last words could be heard for miles—well not really, but that was the intent. "I hope our plane is on schedule. I can't wait to see my family!" Sara announced to the world.

On the way to the airport, Gram confided to Sara that Anne informed her Linc, Martha, Martin, and Leanne were all leaving for home in three days—not the original three weeks they had previously planned. The change in plan was for security reasons. Now they might be leaving the same day as Sara and Gram.

True to the Ambassador's word, a sky cap walked past to the limousine as they were gathering their luggage.

"Make sure we get his name," Sara cautioned Gram.

She didn't have to say a word. The sky cap returned and made them his next stop.

"Need help with your luggage, ladies?" he questioned without identifying himself.

They stood there like two dummies, thinking perhaps they should send him away.

"I'm Ted, by the way, at your service."

Phew, problem solved. Everything else went as planned. Ted pushed their dolly with the luggage up to the departing gate. Gram tipped him and he left. The plane for EWR was announced. They were told to go to the gate and board when the final section was called, making sure they were last. At this point they felt Gaeta was no longer on their itinerary. How in the world could they not board the plane?

They handed over their tickets and went through the open door leading to the plane passage. Before they took two steps, another door opened and Ted appeared, motioning them to follow him. Sara had flown many times and had never noticed a door like that. They were led down a hall into a room. Ted told them airline personnel used this area to get to a plane without going through the gate.

Another shock was waiting in this room. The woman and young girl from the Rome airport were there, dressed in the same clothes they wore at the last exchange. As Sara and Gram entered the room, the duplicates left, reversing the path just taken. Gram and Sara went out of the room, following Ted out another door, down some steps, and outside to a small vehicle similar to a golf cart, except it had windows impossible to see into from the outside.

At this point they lost Ted. The driver drove them far from the departing plane to an area accommodating private jets. After they boarded a jet whose lone emblem was an Italian flag, the sleek bird took off. Less than a half hour later, Gaeta was back on the itinerary.

It was a small airport, so Sara imagined their next escort had little trouble recognizing them. He introduced himself with enough information, proving he was legit. After a short ride, a lovely vision called Gaeta appeared. Gaeta is a city that rises from the ocean straight up to the mountain summit.

The driver pulled up to a very old but beautiful building with stunning ancient architecture. The color of the building's stucco and the sun melded into one. The name of this lovely inn was MilleQuarcento. One of the owners greeted them in perfect English and a smile that spelled welcome. The building was originally constructed in the 15th century and was in the perfect location, with its sweeping view of the city culminating right down to the ocean. The center of Gaeta was a mere two kilometers from the inn; the ocean was four kilometers away. Everything was within walking distance.

Their room was not a room at all, but a suite consisting of two bedrooms with connecting bathrooms, separated by a sitting room revealing floor-to-ceiling windows displaying a magnificent view. Each bedroom had lovely canopied beds. The bathrooms were state-of-the-art modern, with neutral colors that seemed to bring the outside atmosphere indoors. A deep blue-and-yellow porcelain bowl filled with fruit, hard crackers, olives, and small biscotti brought a vivid splash of color to the overall soft earth-tone decor. It sat on an antique table that had two matching chairs.

They decided those delectable treats would be perfect for lunch. The fruit here was so much better than the homeland variety. Gram poured from a small bottle of wine labeled "Greco," calling the liquid "nectar from the gods." Things were really looking better.

Gram was anxious to show Sara the sights that she and Grandpa had visited. They unpacked and, with maps in hand, took off.

34 EXPLORING MENTALLY AND PHYSICALLY

Later, they took a short walk downhill on a cobblestone street in blistering heat. At the bottom of the hill, they found the beginning of the main street in Gaeta, Indipendenze Plaza. Blocks of attached two-story buildings loomed in front of them. Not a soul appeared on the streets. The buildings were solidly closed, and shutters blocked any signs of windows. Sara compared it to a Western ghost town. She was so thirsty, but drinks were nowhere in sight. The ocean was always in front of them as they walked. A Samuel Coleridge poem Sara remembered from an English class triggered a parched throat: "Water, water everywhere, nor any drop to drink." The line was from *The Albatross*. It's amazing how useless knowledge is when you're dying of thirst.

Sara's great grandmother's address had been 90 Indipendenze Plaza. It was quite a walk to that building. Fortunately, before they started out, they found a small store hidden in a tiny alley, and they were able to buy water there. The store was reminiscent of a 7-Eleven.

Once Sara's thirst was quenched, her attitude changed. Now she was anxious to see the building where this lady from long ago had grown up. Finally they reached 90 Indipendenze. The building was similar to all the others, but suddenly it had a special aura that turned into mental pictures in Sara's mind. Before her eyes, a girl her own age came out the door and down the few steps leading to the street. She stopped at the bottom and turned back toward the house as if waiting for someone.

"I know who you are, Theresa Albani. You are a part of me. We are just separated by generations." Sara's innermost thoughts screamed to be heard but remained silent, private to her alone.

The mental images became quite vivid, not typical of anything she had ever experienced. The girl wore an ankle-length skirt made of coarse material like the dish towels at home. The dark, drab colors seemed equally unattractive. Her blouse had short sleeves edged in simple embroidery. Her thick, dark red hair, which was pulled to one side with a single braid, reached below her waist.

The door opened and a woman Sara assumed to be Theresa's mother descended the steps. She was dressed in a long, drab plaid skirt and a white blouse with embroidery, like the girl's except that it had long sleeves. She joined her daughter and they strolled down the street holding hands. Sara could feel their entwined love.

"Sara, I've been talking to you but you were someplace else. What were you thinking about?" Gram asked.

Suddenly, Sara was back in the present and the images disappeared. She tried to explain what had just happened to Gram, describing the two women as they appeared in the vision. When she described the girl's braid, a strange expression crossed Gram's face.

"Your great grandmother, Theresa, had that braid you described. When she had her first haircut, the braid was cut off and she saved it. I know because she showed it to me. How do you know their clothing style? Have you seen pictures of the way they dressed?"

Sara had never seen pictures of that time or place. In

fact, she had never had any interest in the past. Now she wanted to know everything about these two. Unfortunately, Gram didn't have much information about them.

After a few moments Gram did something very unusual for a woman who would never trespass. She climbed the three steps leading to the front door and touched the knob, expecting it to be locked. Surprisingly, it wasn't. The door opened, revealing a long, steep stairway.

"Gram, I'm going up those steps to see the rooms where they lived."

"Sara, I don't think that's wise. It's private property." After a long pause, Gram added, "But it seems so important to you. Sometimes rules are meant to be bent. I'll stay right here until you come down. Call if you want me to come up."

Sara climbed those stairs as if knowing they were going to reveal some connection to the past. When she got inside, the apartment was bare of furniture. It was obvious that it was being prepared for new tenants as the walls were freshly painted and the bathroom and kitchen had been updated. The only things that were not new were two wall sconces in the living room. They were brass, with ornate decorations, and the light bulbs were in the shape of candles. Sara stared at those sconces, knowing she had seen them many times, but she couldn't zero in on where. The clear distinction between long ago and the present had become unclear, a maze filled with a confusing assortment of facts, missing a placement in time.

As Sara walked toward the steps to leave, she heard a man with an accent talking to Gram as they both climbed the stairs. Arriving at the top of the steps, Gram introduced Sara to Victor, the realtor for the apartment.

With his broken English, he chatted away in a friendly manor. Not once did he mention that Sara was a trespasser, for which she was most grateful. He told them that the last renters had just moved out and he was readying the place for new tenants.

Sara and Gram filled Victor in on why this apartment was so fascinating to them. Sara found herself doing an about turn on her interest in her great grandparents. A few days ago, finding out about relatives from the past was not very high on her interest scale. Now she was a veritable sponge soaking up any bit of information about the Albani family history, as if something were drawing her to this part of her past. Strange!

She could see Gram didn't quite understand her new captivation. It was off the wall to Sara as well. If only generations didn't separate people, connections with the past would never be broken.

Victor offered the limited information he had about the past. He knew there were still Albani and Dischino families in Gaeta but suggested they visit the Tourist Bureau for more information. They might be able to open more doors.

If Sara had her way, the next stop would be the Tourist Bureau. Gram suggested putting that off until tomorrow morning, when they had a full day to follow through with research if they wanted to do that.

Turning back to Victor, Gram said, "You have been so helpful. We apologize for trespassing. Fortunately, you speak English so beautifully and understood our curiosity. Now I'm wondering if I might ask you for one more bit of information. Do you have any suggestions for dinner?"

"Try Antico Forno Giordano. People from everywhere eat there. It is famous for its tiella. It's really good. I don't know the exact address, but it's right on Indipendenze Plaza. The number, I think, is in the 30s. Where are you staying?"

"At MilleQuarcento," Gram replied.

"That's really nice. Antico is on your way back. Just follow Indipendenze. It will be across the street. Please tell them Victor Erda spoke to you. Arrivederci."

"Ciao, Victor, and thanks again."

35 THE PAST INTERTWINES WITH THE PRESENT

"Gram, one more thing before we go," Sara added as she walked over to the wall with the sconces. "Where have I seen these before?"

A look of total amazement replaced simple curiosity on Gram's face. "I didn't even notice them. Sara, those are exactly the same as the ones in our entrance. Your great grandparents had them in their bedroom. We always admired them. After they died, we took them out of the house before we sold it. So there must have been four of them in this room at one time."

Gram called to Victor, who was already halfway down the stairs, and asked him to come back up.

"Victor, I know you're in a hurry, but I just noticed those sconces. I have a matching pair in my home."

Even Victor, who had no connection to their family, was suddenly engaged by this bit of information.

In that moment, Gram had an idea. She had a lovely home and certainly didn't need any decorative additions. In fact, she and Joe were trying to downsize. But the sconces were obviously intriguing.

"Victor, I know this is a somewhat strange question to ask, but I would like to buy those sconces. They are a connection to the past for our whole family. We don't know why Theresa didn't take all four, but I would love to bring these home to Joe, as if his mother were giving him one more gift. What an interesting legacy it would be. I would also buy reasonably priced replacements. Would you consider selling them?"

Victor didn't reply right away. He wanted to do and say the right thing. "I have no problem with your idea. The owner lives in Milan and only cares about the apartment being rented. You are the only people with a connection to those sconces. I think they were electrified in the 1930s. They were gas lamps before that. I'm sure the new renters, whoever they may be, couldn't care less. I can pick up very nice modern ones as replacements. Would $100 for the two seem reasonable?"

Gram thought about how much she and Joe had paid for antiques in the past. This price was quite reasonable.

"Great, Victor! I really appreciate this. I will give you $150 for the sconces and their replacements. Now, how do we get these home?"

Again Victor paused. It took a bit of planning to sort out the best procedure. "I have an apartment to show in half an hour and then I'm leaving for Rome for the weekend. I will pick up the replacements on Monday."

"Oh, unfortunately, we are leaving on Sunday for Rome and flying home on Monday."

Sara mentally reviewed the possibilities. "There are several boxes in the bedroom. One looks the right size. Is there any way we could take these sconces up to our hotel now and then get someone to ship them to the US?"

"Sara, that's not a bad idea. I can cut holes around the sconces in the wall, and then I really have to go. Let me call two of my nephews to carry the scones to your hotel."

Victor got on his cell phone while Gram took out the Euros to pay for her purchase. She even included an extra

$25 for his help.

"It will take an hour for my nephews to get here. Will that work?"

Sara and Gram had no problem with that, so Victor used a hammer and a sharp pick from a kitchen drawer and began to cut through the wall around the sconces. They were attached to old wiring that hadn't seen the light of day in almost a century. The heavy wiring kept the lighting from sliding to the floor.

"If you just keep pulling on that wiring, the plug to which it is attached will come up. I've seen lots of these in the old buildings. I've turn off the electricity. Just disconnect it, but please make sure you leave the end of the wires outside the wall. Don't let them drop back in. If you run into trouble, my nephews should be able to help you. Also, here is my cell phone number. I really have to go now. Ciao."

With that, Victor took two steps at a time down the stairway and vanished out the door.

"Hope we can do this, Sara."

It was getting so hot in the room. There was a small window air conditioner, but, unfortunately, the electricity was turned off. The two attacked the job full steam. They had to be ready for the men in less than an hour. Each loosened a sconce from the wall and began to pull and pull. Yards of wiring tied with narrow wire seemed to go on forever. Finally, each pulled out the plug to which her sconce was attached.

Gram's came out easily. Pulling it out until it reached the floor, she said, "Sara, I'm afraid these wires will fall back into the wall. Can you hold this while I look for something to hold them down to the floor?"

"Gram, there are paint cans galore in the bedroom. One of them would probably hold it."

Gram discovered two perfect-sized cans heavy enough to prevent the wires from disappearing into the wall. She put the wires under the can, and they seemed quite secure.

When she finished, she went to help Sara, who was having some trouble.

"Gram, I have the connection plug, but I think something is attached to the wires below. I'm really afraid that if I don't get whatever is down there out, the wire will fall back into the wall."

Sara pulled more and then stopped. A material bag of some sort was plugging the hole. It was obvious the hole had to be enlarged before whatever was there could be released. Gram retrieved the pick Victor had used and worked at making the hole larger. Finally, Sara was able to pull the bag out of the wall. It was made of coarse, dark dress material. They released the bag and pulled out enough wire to reach the floor. Then they used a second can of paint to hold the wires from slipping back into the wall.

The bag was difficult to open as it had been sewn together tightly by hand. Before they could get the bag open, they heard a door opening and voices uttering "hallo," indicating the nephews were there.

"Let's put that bag in the box with the sconces and we'll look at it when we get to the hotel," Gram suggested.

The nephews, who were both around 20, were most friendly. Gram asked them to take the box and leave it at the front desk of their inn. She told them to go ahead to the inn, since she was going to make reservations at the restaurant Victor had suggested. Gram gave the young men some money to buy something cool to drink on their way.

After making sure they locked the door as Victor had asked them to do, the tired travelers left 90 Indipendenze Plaza. It was so hot when they left the apartment that the short walk to the restaurant left them wilting.

Most of the shops were still boarded up, but a door displaying the restaurant's name was open. After a few minutes, a young man appeared at the small entrance. Fortunately, he spoke some English, and he took a reservation for eight o'clock, promising them un pasto delizioso ("a delicious meal").

It was mid-afternoon when they reached their hotel. They were beat and ended up falling sound asleep in their chairs while watching the European CNN. Before Sara drifted off, the word *Embassy* was mentioned, but sleep blocked any further information.

36 GAETA DISPLAYS HER CHARMS

By the time they woke up from their nap, they realized there was only an hour before their dinner reservation. Each of them had her own bathroom, so dressing was easy. They decided to primp a bit. Sara wore a frothy blue sleeveless dress accessorized with some newly bought costume jewelry. The heels might be a walking problem, but it was fashion at all costs! Gram had a cool lime green sundress, and she was taking no chances with heels.

"If we're too tired to walk back, I'm sure the restaurant will call a taxi for us," Gram suggested, knowing how the heat could wear them down. The walk was less than a mile, but in the sweltering heat it was daunting.

With water bottles and cameras stashed in their bags, they hoped they had made the proper preparations. It was a little after seven, and they noted the temperature had dropped pleasantly.

With all the adventures they had recently shared, conversation was never a problem. They chatted, laughed, and then pondered over Sara's strange visions at the apartment on Indipendenze. In Sara's mind there was still confusion over reality and the visions that seemed so real, but they didn't dwell on that too long. Before they knew it, that special street came up.

An unbelievable transformation had been created on Via Indipendenze! The dark boarded-up buildings were now alive with people and activity. It had become a street mall! The wooden doors had been lifted from the first floor of many of the buildings after siesta, and now they welcomed business. The counters were laden with fresh, gleaming vegetables and fruits of every description and color: green lettuce, yellow squash, red beets, oranges. The sights were overwhelming. Freshly caught fish, or so the proprietors yelled, were on display, still with heads on and eyes staring. Cheese stands offered many varieties to sample or purchase. Chocolates, bakery perfections, and mouth-watering foods were in abundance. Each seller tried to outdo his competitors by shouting out about the quality of his products. Sara frequented farmers' markets near home but had never encountered any like this!

By the time they arrived at Antico Forno Giordano, Sara was starving. All those smells made her stomach growl with the anticipation of a good meal. The restaurant had several benches and two tables. People watching seemed like a fun idea, so she and Gram were quite content to sit at one of the tables outside. There was a counter where people could take out the tasty products, and the line of people waiting proved its popularity. It wasn't a fancy place but certainly seemed to be highly regarded.

The waiter was good looking. Sara did a double take when he came over to welcome them and take their order. He was about 16 and had dark hair and blue eyes, was tall, and spoke English—in other words, he was almost perfection! During his welcoming conversation, which lasted several minutes, he informed them he was the owner's grandson and this was his first summer being a waiter. They asked about the specialty of the house, a famous Gaeton dish called *tiella*. It was like a pie with a top and bottom crust. When you ordered, you chose from a variety of fillings. Sara picked one with several different vegetables, cheese, and tuna fish. Gram's was almost the same except she included anchovies—definitely not Sara's choice!

The Europeans have this wonderful soda called Orangina, which Sara really liked, so she ordered that to go with her meal. Gram chose a local white wine.

The young man was obviously taking too long attending to one table, so a white-haired gentleman poked his head outside the front entrance. Their waiter was gone in a flash!

It was a blast watching all the goings on in this lively city. The waiter, whose name was Cosmos, was at their table whenever he wasn't busy, but he kept his eye on the front door! They asked this charming young man his top choices of places to visit in a two-day time frame. He promised to make a list before they left.

When the food came, Sara would have enjoyed almost anything. That's how hungry she was. The tiella was so good. The crust was flaky and the filling so well combined that it was hard to identify separate items, but the total taste was to die for. If she was on death row having to pick a last meal, tiella would rank high on Sara's list. That's how good it was. Of course, chatting with the blue-eyed waiter enhanced the flavor.

When the meal had been savored to the last bite, true to his word, Cosmos had a list of "musts" to see. While Gram paid the bill, Sara, wanting to extend the conversation a bit longer, mentioned her new interest in doing an ancestry search on her great grandmother. Cosmos suggested trying the court house. At that moment, the white-haired gentleman reappeared with a look of annoyance that said "get back to work."

"That's my grandfather. I've got to go. Hope I see you again." His eyes were directed straight at Sara.

37 FANTASY AND REALITY CROSS SWORDS

While exploring the numerous alleys that were appendages to the Plaza, they came across a newsstand. Noticing newspaper headlines including the word *Embassy*, they bought a paper and took it back to the hotel, where someone could translate the article for them. Sara saw a T-shirt in orange that said Gaeta on it. Believe it or not, it had a baseball emblem on it. Since baseball was AJ's sport, it seemed the perfect gift for him.

They walked until they were in front of 90 Indipendenze Plaza, Sara's great grandmother's childhood home. There was a small café across the street that displayed a variety of gelato, all very appetizing. This was dessert and the two quickly made choices. Fortunately, they saw two empty bistro tables with chairs.

Every scrumptious morsel of those frozen delights was evidence that Gaetons knew how to eat. The sense of being transported to another time that Sara had experienced in the afternoon came slowly back, taking over the present. The young girl with the long red braid was sitting in Gram's seat. She wasn't eating but sipping a tiny cup of coffee, maybe espresso. It was as if she were trying to make it last. A somewhat younger boy walked up to her, pointing to her cup. She shook her head, and he walked away annoyed. Food must have been in short supply for them.

Sara pushed what was left of her gelato toward her.

"Are you finished, Sara?"

"Are you done, Sara?"

"Sara, where are you?"

Sara snapped back to reality, noting it was Gram sitting next to her, not the girl. It was impossible to keep this new and bizarre experience to herself. It wasn't an unpleasant episode; it was just "wacko," as her grandpa called anything out of the ordinary.

While walking back to the inn, Sara unfolded her latest experience. When she shared the image of a boy approaching the young girl and touching her cup, Gram interrupted, "Theresa had an older brother as well as a younger one. The older one was Joe; the younger was Salvatore.

"The family was very poor. That's why everyone came to America. Joe arrived in America with his father first. I know they all settled in or near Somerville, Massachusetts. Sara, this is really strange. I know you are absolutely honest in what you are telling me. You never heard any of their history. Your visions are, frankly, unexplainable but fascinating. I hope you are writing all this down in your journal."

Sara assured her all this was in writing. Truthfully, her journal had only a few blank pages left. She really needed a new one.

Right before they turned the corner to go up the hill to the inn, Sara spotted a lovely small shop selling cards, stationery, and books. After looking up the Italian word for *journal*, Sara found a leather one with olives encircling the word *giornale* on the cover. She was delighted to see a map of Gaeta inside. She bought that, along with the

English version of a book entitled *Gaeta, City of Charm*. It had umpteen pictures and descriptions of this attractive town that now held a sense of magnetism for her. Along with her many photos, this book was a nice memento.

Their room was a welcome sight after a long day, with its soft neutral colors speckled with an evening glow. After writing her daily email updates to family and friends, Sara skimmed through her newly purchased book. There were places begging to be explored, if time would allow.

As she closed the book, the author's name caught her attention: Vincent Albani. Wow, wasn't that a familiar name? Gram was stunned as well. On the last page there was a blurb about the author. He actually lived in Gaeta, or rather a tiny town located on the outskirts. When they Googled his name, they found information about him, including his website.

"Why don't you email him? He might be able to help you add insight to your search. It wouldn't hurt to try." Gram's suggestion was right on.

Sara's fingers flew as she typed a brief note about herself, including her great grandmother's maiden name. As the email headed for cyberspace, she yearned for a quick response. Time was so limited. One more day and Gaeta would become a memory. Just as Sara sent the email, there was a knock on their door. One of the hotel attendants brought the box that had been delivered by Victor's nephews. The exhausted tourists had completely forgotten it.

Gram set the box on a table. The bag, with its coarse material and tightly sewn stitches, seemed not to want to give away its long-hidden secrets. And the years inside the wall had contributed a moldy, unpleasant smell that hit them in the face as soon as they opened the box.

"Yuck, that bag is disgusting. Maybe we should just throw it away. It's probably loaded with germs," Sara said as she turned her head away from the box and crinkled up her nose.

"Sara, where is your sense of curiosity? Somebody went to a lot of effort to hide this," Gram offered.

"Well, okay. You open it. I'm standing far away. Do you have something to open it?"

"Not really. I'll try with the knife we've used for fruit. I keep it in my bag."

Gram struggled with the knife, making little headway loosening the tight stitches. After some time, she went to the lobby and told them she needed to cut some heavy material. A woman from Housekeeping gave her scissors similar to wire cutters. Gram put those heavy buggers to work, finally cutting across the top of the bag.

When she turned the bag upside down, tiny delicately sewn bags spilled onto the table. The material was much finer than the larger bag. There must have been 25 or more of those little packages. Gram shook the larger bag until it was obvious that all the little bags had fallen out. These were followed by unopened mildewed envelopes. One last item concealed inside the larger bag was a sealed envelope with the words *danaro per l'america* ("money to America") written on the outside.

Opening the envelope seemed as daunting as opening the bag. So many years had almost obliterated what was written on it, and the smell was really bad.

Finally, Gram managed to remove the letter and open it gingerly. It appeared to be an itemized accounting of some repeated activity. Holding her nose, Sara peered at the deteriorated sheets.

Salvatore Albani—30 lira Settembre scambio florin
Theresa Albani—10 lira Settembre scambio florin
Joe Albani—40 dollars Settembre, america scambio florin
Giovanni Albani—40 dollars Settembre, america scambio florin
Maria Albani—5 dollars Settembre, america scambio florin

"It looks like a list of people's names and then an amount for each person," Sara guessed. "Each name is repeated many times with different months and amounts."

"This must have been what each family member contributed to the family goal to come to America," Gram suggested. "I don't know what *scambio* or *florin* means, though."

Sara pulled out her miniature Italian dictionary. "*Scambio* means 'to change or exchange.'" After a moment, she added, "A *florin* is an old gold coin."

"GOLD!" they shouted simultaneously.

Both of them ran to their makeup bags, grabbed a small scissors, and then started snipping at the small material packages, exposing their contents. Various amounts of beautiful gold coins spilled out of the bags, glistening as if they had never been hidden. They kept opening bags and dropping the contents on the table until all the containers were cleared of their booty.

All the two could do was stare at each other, speechless. This was beyond words. It was so unreal—like an unbelievable movie that you would laugh at because it was so unrealistic.

Recovery came slowly. The realization that they were the sole possessors of a possible fortune created questions and the dilemma of what to do.

"Gram, whose coins are these?"

"They belonged to your great grandmother's family. There are accounts going on for several years, according to that list. It may not have been a fortune in the early 1900s, but I think it is now. Why the bag wasn't discovered when they electrified the sconces I don't know."

Sara noted that the bag was positioned quite a bit below the electric connection. The ancestors probably had no idea of electricity and its uses when they hid the bag in the wall.

"Sara, they must have intended to take the gold to America to live on. Why they didn't take it is a mystery."

PJ DISCHINO

"Maybe somehow they took the wrong sconces. You have two at your house," Sara suggested.

"That's right. Let's talk this over slowly and try to get a handle on it," Gram proposed.

Sara wondered who should have ownership of this money at the present time.

"It's family money. It was meant to help the family survive."

"But who are the living descendants?" Sara asked.

Gram pondered that one. "Well, that would be Grandpa, his children and grandchildren, all six of you, his living sister and her son, his dead sister's two girls, grandchildren . . . I think that's it."

"What are we going to do with it?"

"Let's think about it. I feel it's money that belongs to the family. I would like to bring it home and give it to Grandpa, hire a lawyer, and do what is legally fair."

"I think you're right. But how will we get it there?"

After a lengthy pause, Gram offered a plan.

38 A SOLUTION FROM THE PAST

"During the age of immigration in the early 20th century, the voyagers traveling to America from Europe were afraid that the little money they had would be taken away from them, so they took their gold coins and sewed them into the hems of skirts. The material was usually heavy anyway, so the coins would go unnoticed. Our clothes are much lighter than theirs were, but the coins are tiny. Should we try doing the same thing they did?" Gram suggested.

Sara thought it was a perfect idea. It took them quite awhile to execute their plan. With tiny nail scissors, they would cut just enough stitches in their own hems to slide the tiny coins and move them in a position to keep them from slipping out. Then Gram squeezed a drop of her sewing glue into each bit of seam that was open. Finally, all the treasure was stowed away.

Sara suggested they use a hair dryer to dry a little bit of the bag and paper from the letter and envelope, hoping these items wouldn't totally disintegrate. Her idea was genius! The material dried, and the smell almost disappeared. Then they carefully dried the letter using the lowest heat. The paper seemed dry but fragile. They slid it into a gallon-size baggie, squeezing as much air out as possible before sealing it. It was as readable as it had ever been. They did this with every paper item. Some envelopes were still unopened.

"I have no idea about the value of these coins, but they must be worth something. After all, the family members were going to use the money for their journey and for their new life in America. I just can't imagine why they didn't take it," Gram repeated.

At this point Sara was so emotionally drained she could hardly think. Her head pounded. She was in the midst of a whirlwind of discovery. The unexpected was now the expected

The day's activity had exhausted them both, and their beds were calling to them. As they closed their eyes, sleep immediately erased the confusion.

Hmmmm . . . . Never assume!

39 TENSIONS REKINDLE

The inn served breakfast Continental style, with flaky pastries and a pot of hot chocolate that was certainly not instant! While they ate, Gram and Sara considered climbing Mount Orlando. After all, Cosmos had listed it as a must! There was a 562 foot drop from the top right down to the Mediterranean, offering an unbelievable view. Gram felt the climb might be too much for her but was determined Sara should see it.

After breakfast, they checked at the front desk and discovered an English-speaking tour was leaving at 10:00. In addition to climbing the mountain, the tour included a visit to the Plano Mausoleum, which was now a museum.

Sara assured Gram that it would be perfect.

"I don't know how I feel about not being with you after some of our unpleasant experiences . . ." Gram began.

The owner of the inn, who was handling the desk, overhead her and interrupted, "The tours are very well conducted, and there are usually several Americans on each tour as Gaeta has an American Naval Base. If you choose to go, a van will pick you up here. The hike up to the top of Orlando is certainly not difficult for someone of your age, Sara."

Gram relented after being assured Sara would call her from her cell frequently. The owner called the tour group to add Sara. There were 20 people, including Sara, on the tour, and two American families would be part of the group.

It was 8:30 now, so that left plenty of time to get ready. There were small shops on the narrow street where the inn was located. Gram suggested they take a look. Most were closed, but they discovered one that was open, with people sitting at bistro tables having coffee. They sat down at a table and ordered some cool drinks.

Sara noticed that an English newspaper had been left on their table. A headline in the middle of the front page caught her eye: "AMERICAN EMBASSY ACCUSED OF HARBORING FUGITIVE." She immediately moved her chair next to Gram's so they could read the article together. It went on to say that the fugitive was a very important individual from a country not friendly to the Western world. There was speculation that certain people from that country would stop at nothing to capture or even destroy this person. The article continued, but what they had already read was enough for them.

Sara's inner turmoil returned big time. But the young often rise to the occasion. They don't know any better. And Gram's lack of panic was a buoy. How she remained calm, Sara had no idea.

Actually, Gram's peaceful manner was only on the surface. If she had been traveling with Joe or by herself, she would be in a panic now. But she was the one who had asked her granddaughter to join her, and it was her responsibility to not only provide a safe return but also to promote a sense of adventure with security on the trip, not to cause fear and fright. Gram's whole being shook internally, but she reminded herself that today should be free from unwanted tension. After all, the trouble was in Rome. No one knew about Gaeta.

Sara was glad she had told Gram the whole story before leaving Rome. Now they were both on the same page. The thought that the Balsalm family would be in trouble distressed them, but they weren't concerned about their own safety as they were out of that situation now.

"Let's go back to the room, and I'll email Linc to see if he can tell us anything," Sara suggested.

When they were almost to the inn, Sara noticed a man dressed in dark slacks and jacket. He caught her eye because he looked out of place. Most people were wearing cool summer clothes due to the heat. He looked somewhat familiar, but she'd only gotten a brief glance so she couldn't really tell. Before he turned a corner and was out of sight, Gram noticed him too and mentioned how his clothes were so warm for all this heat.

Sara wrote a quick email to Linc. She did take time to attach some photos of the inn and last night's restaurant, though. There was much more to say, but she mainly wanted to know if they were all safe.

As she pressed "Send," another email was coming in. It was a response from Vincent Albani, the author of the Gaeta book. He told her to visit him anytime at his book store. She couldn't believe the store number: 93 Indipendenze Plaza. It was right across the street from her great grandmother's apartment!

She and Gram decided that tomorrow morning would be a good time to stop at Vincent's book store. It was getting close to 10:00 now, and Sara had to join the tour. She said goodbye to Gram and left.

Walking out the front door of the inn, Sara saw a fairly large group. She went up to a woman and asked if this was the tour for Mount Orlando and was assured it was. From her accent, Sara realized the woman was one of the American members of the tour. They were just getting acquainted when two vans arrived and parked. The tour guides explained one tour would be in English while the other would be in Italian. The English-speaking group was actually made up of ten Americans. They found seats in the proper van and strapped themselves into seats in the blissfully air-conditioned vehicle. It was already 30 degrees Celsius, and it was only 10:00.

From her seat in the van, Sara could see the café where they had read the paper. A chill went through her when she noticed the man who was dressed so improperly. He was sitting at a table reading the newspaper but had his eyes on her van. This time she could see his full face, and she realized that he was one of the men who had been talking to Simon outside the Balsalms' villa in Rome. There was no question in her mind that this was the same man. Should she leave the tour and rush to tell Gram? Before she could decide what to do, the van pulled away from the inn. Sara tried to convince herself this was her imagination working overtime.

40 GREAT TOUR, HOWEVER . . .

As the van made its way to its destination, the guide, a man around 25, filled them in on Gaetian history. The vehicle followed the path up Mt. Orlando, and then the tourists had to walk up a fairly steep hill to view the Mausoleum of Munazio Planco. The mausoleum dominated the view and was visible from as far away as Formia. It was featured in many photos of the Gulf of Gaeta that were included in books about its history. Sara was impressed that the building was famous because it had managed to retain its outer covering when so many other monuments had failed. It was among the best preserved of the mausoleums in Italy. And the view of the bay was gorgeous.

Thankfully, the hike back down the hill was a lot easier than the climb up. Everyone piled into the van for the last stop and lunch.

Serapo beach was a perfect ending, so popular because of the very fine sand and the crystalline sea of the Tyrrhenian Coast. Every spot was filled with blue-and-white rental chairs dotting the pristine beach. Lunch was served on the wide porch of a restaurant facing the sea. The waiter brought small bowls of olives, a Gaetian specialty. Normally Sara avoided olives, but these weren't too bad. She enjoyed the lunch as she recapped the tour with her American companions, and the view was a feast for the eyes.

At 3:30 Sara was back at the inn, pleased to have taken the tour. She rushed inside to tell Gram all about it. Sara had forgotten to check in with her and hoped that it hadn't caused a problem.

As she passed through the lobby, the inn proprietor called to her. "Sara, your grandmother told us all about your visit with Vincent Albani tomorrow. Perhaps you may be related. To bring you up to date, Mr. Albani called and invited you and your grandmother to his house for dinner tonight. He is sending a car for you at 5:00. Your grandmother went out to the florist down the block to find an appropriate gift to bring along. She said you should go ahead and get dressed and she will meet you in the room."

Sara went up to her room. By 4:45 she had showered and dressed for the evening. Gram still wasn't back. How long did it take to buy flowers? She didn't dwell on that point, as 5:00 was fast approaching. Sara was excited to meet Vincent Albani. Family history held little importance previously, but now it was an obsession with her. Those realistic visions she'd had of the past left her wanting to know more about that young girl and her family.

Five minutes later, she wondered again where Gram was. Why wasn't she here? How long could it have possibly taken her to buy flowers? Hopefully, she was in the lobby or out front waiting for her, but Sara had an uneasy feeling.

The lobby was empty, so she hurried to the front door. Still no Gram. As she opened the door, she noticed a man dressed in a chauffeur's uniform directly outside. He asked her if her name was Sara. After getting an affirmative answer, he said he was the driver for the evening and that Gram was already inside the limousine parked in the back.

Sara was so glad to know Gram was nearby. She followed the driver without hesitation, but she couldn't see the limo.

"The car is parked in that garage." He pointed to an unattached building somewhat hidden from view.

When he opened the garage door, he roughly shoved Sara inside. Two other men were waiting there. One of them had a white cloth in his hand. She recognized them as the other men who had been talking with Simon outside the Roman villa. One of them was the man she'd seen outside the café this morning.

The car door opened. Sara froze as a familiar man stepped out. The sight of Simon caused a sense of helpless fear that she had never experienced in her short life. At the same moment, her eyes traveled to the back seat of the car. Gram wasn't there, but Martha and Linc were. They were asleep—or could they be dead?

41 DAYTIME NIGHTMARE

The man with the white cloth handed it to Simon, who grabbed Sara's arm and tried to cover her nose and mouth with it. The sickening odor was overwhelming. Before he got a chance to cover her mouth completely, she wrenched herself free. Seeing a shovel with a pointed end propped up within reach against the garage wall, she grabbed it. With all her might, Sara directed the point right into his stomach. Because of the heat, he was wearing a thin dress shirt. The shovel went through it as if it were tissue paper and found its mark well into his gut, causing blood to spurt out like a volcano erupting. His scream of agony caused the other two men to completely forget about Sara as they rushed to Simon's aid.

The garage door was closed, but Sara noticed a window, which was, unfortunately, locked. Sara had her bag with her iPad in it, ready to take notes at Victor Albani's store. Using the bag, she smashed at the window until the glass and the frame were broken. It only took a few seconds.

The blood was still gushing from Simon's wound. The men were so preoccupied and shocked by the turn of events that they were oblivious to anything else. She made one fast exit through that window, landing on the ground outside.

As Sara got up, she looked at her sleeve, which was quickly becoming soaked with blood. A good-sized piece of bloody broken glass lying on the ground next to her was the obvious cause.

As she tried to run for help, nausea and light-headedness made it impossible for her to move quickly. Whatever was on that white cloth had definitely affected her.

Stumbling to the street, Sara realized this was not Indipendenze but a totally unfamiliar street. She noticed a large building enclosed by a fence. A gate with a smaller building was at one end, and a uniformed attendant sat inside. It must be the American Naval Base that had been pointed out on her Mt. Orlando Tour.

She managed to reach the gate, even though she was feeling more and more incapacitated. The guard quickly realized she was in trouble. He opened the door to his little sanctuary and offered her a seat. Sara blurted out the situation in as few words as possible, not only because action was needed immediately but also because she felt so terribly ill. He was an American, so there was no confusion about what she had said; and he responded immediately when he heard the words Embassy, Ambassador Balsalm, children, and Gram. He handed Sara a bottle of water while he picked up his phone and made a call.

The building was immediately surrounded by uniformed men. They asked question upon question; but at this point, Sara was so sick that she could barely answer them.

She closed her eyes for a few moments. When she opened them again, she noticed a group of naval men standing a distance away. Then the door of the small booth opened. It was one of Simon's men. All Sara saw was a revolver pointed directly at her before a curtain of darkness blackened out reality.

42 THE SITUATION BECOMES DESPERATE

Sara kept fighting to crawl out of the darkness, a slow and torturous process. The more she became aware of her surroundings, the more the pounding in her head felt like an unbearable tightening clamp. Consciousness brought about a dreadful realization. She was in terrible pain and horrific danger.

Slowly opening her eyes, Sara realized why every bone in her body felt racked with pain. She was lying on a cement floor. There was also a putrid smell stagnating every breath she took.

Raising her head, she thought, "I must have been here a long time. There's blood and vomit all over, and I can't move."

She heard weeping coming from a room nearby, along with a comforting male voice.

"Oh God! Linc and Martha are close by and they are in trouble too!"

After trying to move for several minutes, she realized she was stiff from lying on that hard cement floor for so long. She couldn't determine what was causing her headache, though. She wondered if she'd been hit on the head.

Her body slowly regained some mobility as she tried repeatedly to change positions. After much squirming and stretching, Sara attempted to get up. But she quickly decided to stay put and act unconscious when she heard approaching voices. The conversation was an angry one, carried on in a language totally unfamiliar to her.

Abruptly, the steps stopped, and Sara figured they were in another room. The sobbing and the soothing voice she had heard before ceased. Whatever happened to Martha and Linc certainly wasn't good.

Suddenly, the footsteps and angry voices resumed. Terrified, Sara realized they were approaching her. To the men who entered the room, her eyes appeared to be closed, but she could see three men standing over her. There must have been some discussion of her appearance and odor, as their voices denoted disgust. One of the men was holding the white cloth used on her earlier. More discussion followed. Sara wondered if they were deciding whether or not to use the cloth again.

In a second everything changed. A loud noise came from somewhere else in the building, she presumed. It was deafening and startled the men. They all ran out of her room, leaving the door wide open.

Her instinct for self-preservation took over as Sara struggled to get up, escape her captors, and get help. Staggering weakly through the open door and into a hall, she reached another nearby door that, fortunately, was unlocked. Sara was relieved to find it led to a street.

"I need to know the number of this building and the street to tell people where Linc and Martha are," Sara thought as she left.

The street was totally unfamiliar, but the building had a faded sign that read "Lombardo's Piazza o Mercato, 16 Oceano Avueue." She was still groggy and didn't have anything to write with, so Sara could only hope she wouldn't forget this information.

The area was deserted as far as she could see. Stumbling along the walk with no idea of the direction in which she was headed, Sara saw a bench ahead. Two people were sitting together talking. As she approached them, they were taken aback by the sight of her. They got up quickly, trying to get out of her way.

Sara screamed out the few words she knew in Italian, asking them to stop and help her. Whether they were frozen with fear or realized she was a child, mercifully, they did stop.

Sara saw they were holding a newspaper. She grabbed it and pointed to the article she had read that morning. "Ambassador, penna, scrivere."

The frightened woman reached in her purse and handed her a pen. Sara wrote the address and pointed at the same time to the newspaper. At this point, she was so weak that she had to sit down on the bench. She didn't even notice the couple leaving.

43 PEACE RETURNS

Although she had no idea how long she'd been sleeping on that bench, when Sara awoke, she realized that she felt much better. She stood up and walked around. Her arm felt fine; there was just a little dried blood. The headache was gone, as well as all the other body aches. She didn't even smell anymore. Her clothes looked fresh, as if she had just put them on.

She had to find Gram and tell her what happened. Within a few minutes of walking, she began to recognize places. There was the store where they bought drinks on their first venture into Gaeta. Next, Indipendenze Plaza came into view. She rushed to find the street that would lead to their inn.

It was early evening, and the street was crowded. Passing building number 90, she wished she could stop there, but she had to find Gram. Then she heard someone calling her name. Turning around, Sara discovered the voice was coming from a small café across from number 90. It was the voice of the young girl from her visions. She wasn't a vision now, but someone Sara could touch.

"Sara, where are you going in such a hurry? Remember me? I'm Theresa Albani."

There seemed nothing strange about the conversation. Sara told Theresa there was a problem and she had to find her grandmother.

"Before you go, Sara, come meet my mother and have something to drink. You look tired."

Suddenly it didn't seem so important to get to Gram. She would find out a lot more by talking with Theresa and her mother than by visiting Vincent Albani. She and Theresa held hands as they crossed the street. It felt so warm and good to be with her. They climbed the stairs and went inside, where a woman stood cooking over a large pot. The smells coming from that stove were so delicious!

Theresa introduced Sara to her mother, who spoke a few words in English. Sara had seen the woman walking with Theresa in her previous visions, but this was definitely not a vision. All her senses were working full time, so it had to be real. The aroma of delicious food, the sight of a room with its sparse furniture, the sound of loving voices from caring women, the warm, smooth feeling when she and Theresa held hands, the cool taste of water that Theresa gave her in a tiny frosted glass. All of these were real.

"My mother is trying to learn English to help her adjust when we go to America, but it is hard for her."

"You speak English so well, Theresa. How do you say 'That smells delicious' in Italian?"

Theresa laughed and said, "Cela sent délicieusement bon."

She tried to repeat that to Theresa's mother. It brought the warmest smile as she thanked Sara in English.

"Can you stay for dinner, Sara? The smell comes from my mother's special spaghetti sauce."

"I wish I could, but I have to get to the inn to see Gram."

"Have a cup of espresso before you go," Theresa insisted.

Sara sat down at their wooden kitchen table as Theresa

spread a pretty tablecloth over it and then placed three tiny cups on top. Another plate held several biscotti. Theresa's mother made the espresso one cup at a time in a small copper two-part pot. Sara had never seen anything like this. Everything seemed from another time, but it was all so comforting.

Theresa talked about her father and oldest brother, Joe. They had sailed to America three months earlier, settling in Somerville, Massachusetts, with relatives. When they earned enough money, they would send for the three of them, Theresa, her younger brother Salvatore, and their mother. It would take almost two years to accomplish this.

While listening to the warm conversation, Sara gazed around, wondering why a simple room like this could be so comforting. Then something caught her eye. She couldn't wait to tell Gram that there were four sconces in this room!

Suddenly, Sara could hardly keep her eyes open.

Theresa said with concern, "Sara, you look so tired. Why don't you rest on my bed for a few minutes before you leave? I have a little gift for you too."

Theresa went into another room and brought back a tiny lace bag tied with the narrowest of ribbons. "Here is your present. I hope you will like it," Theresa said as she handed the bag to Sara.

Inside the bag, Sara found three beautifully polished stones.

"These are beach glass. They are formed by broken glass that has spent years being battered by waves. When we find them on the beach, we sand them to a pretty polish. They will bring you good luck."

"Oh thank you. They are lovely, and I will treasure them always. I am so tired. I think I will lie down for a few minutes now."

Theresa led the weary girl to a room with several beds. Sara knew which one was Theresa's as soon as she saw a doll propped up against the pillow.

She put her head on the pillow and Theresa's soft voice lulled her to sleep. "I love you, Sara. Never forget me."

44 CONFUSION

"Sara, wake up! Sara, wake up! Try to open your eyes!"

She heard the words repeated over and over again—the same words coming from different voices. All she wanted was to go back to Gaeta and talk more with Theresa and her mother. Her brother would be home soon and they would eat that delicious food her mother had on the stove. She was so hungry and yet so tired.

"Sara, come on, talk to us."

Another voice.

"Sara, please wake up. I want you to wake up. I miss you."

That voice sounded scared and so familiar. It was her brother AJ, and he needed her.

She tried to open her eyes, but they kept closing. Finally, she realized she was awake, although all she could see were shadows circling around her, shapeless forms. These cloudlike figures made so much noise that they confused her ability to focus on anything.

"She's waking up."

"She keeps blinking her eyes."

"Oh, she's going to be all right."

"It certainly looks that way. Let's all be quiet and give her a chance to realize where she is." That voice sounded professional.

"We have her back, my beautiful Sara." Definitely Mom.

"Hey, Spunda Girl. You're missing out on a lot of fun." Definitely Dad.

"What a journey you have had, Precious Baby Girl." Definitely Gram.

"Time to get up and clean your room." Definitely Grandpa.

"Sara, I want to tell you about some funny commercials on TV." Definitely AJ. He loved certain commercials and could imitate them in a way that always made everyone laugh.

The room was suddenly silent. It was a good thing because these shadowy forms turned into people absolutely spontaneously, as if someone had popped a balloon, leaving Sara back with the people she loved. Everyone was focusing on Sara.

Out of nowhere, a beautiful blonde little girl bounced on the bed and hugged Sara's arm. At first everyone looked shocked, but when a smile appeared on the patient's face, laughter filled the room. Of course, the bouncer was Martha.

Sara had no idea where she was or what had happened. The last thing she remembered before meeting Theresa was trying to get help from the couple sitting on the bench. She tried to think of what to say. Thoughts were hard to formulate.

"I just want to talk to Gram alone. Please."

The room quickly emptied, and Gram stood over Sara, squeezing her hand.

"What a time we've had, Baby Girl. What an adventure! But now you're safe."

"Gram, tell me everything that happened. Where were you?" The questions flowed from her mouth like a verbal waterfall. "But first, can you get me something to eat? I'm starving for spaghetti."

45 MISSING PUZZLE PIECES

"Where are we? What happened to Simon and those men? Where were you? I thought something terrible had happened to Martha and Linc! Why are Mom and Dad here in Gaeta? I just saw Grandpa! I saw AJ. I know I did. Gram, you won't believe what I did to Simon. I probably killed him. Gram, he was going to kill me!"

While Sara was frantically babbling away, a delicious aroma reached her. Simultaneously, Gram picked up her hand, squeezing it with a calming warmth to let her know the danger was over and she was safe. A smiling lady brought in a cart with a gleaming silver-domed dish on top. The luscious smell wafted straight to her growling stomach. She lifted the top and unwrapped a napkin filled with tools to devour a tempting dish of spaghetti.

"Eat slowly, Sara. While you're eating, I'll try to unravel your confusion and fill you in on the details. You alone are responsible for saving the lives of our friends. The Balsalm children would be dead by now if you hadn't gotten help. That couple you mentioned went straight to the police, who reached Martha and Linc without a moment to spare. One of their captors confessed they were about to kill them and then flee the country.

"Simon was seriously injured by your blow with the shovel. He will spend the rest of his life in poor condition in jail. The rest of his accomplices will join him. Their crime is kidnapping, and they will never see the outside world again.

"Of course, they kept blaming each other, but luckily their horrible plan couldn't be executed because of you. They had every intention of killing the entire Balsalm family and anyone else who might get in their way if the refugee at the Embassy was not released to them. We were included in that group."

Sara listened to Gram's account, but her questions were mounting as each detail was opened up. She had only eaten a few mouthfuls and already was full, probably because of not having solid food in a while. How long a while was it?

"Gram, how long was I unconscious? Why were Linc and Martha looking like they were dead? Where were you?" Her questions continued to spill out. She also was so tired that her eyes kept closing, although she wanted Gram to fill in all the gaps.

"Sara, you've been through so much. You need to sleep. I'm going to get something to eat myself. I want you to sleep now."

She barely heard the door shut before her eyelids closed. As she drifted off, she thought about school starting soon, and she was still in Italy. Everyone was in Italy. Sara felt like Alice in Wonderland. "Everything was getting curiouser and curiouser."

46 IT'S ALL SO CONFUSING!

When Sara awoke, Martha was tying the loose strings on her hospital gown into a bow. She was so subdued, not the bouncing Jumping Jack, or rather Jumping Jill, Sara loved.

When Martha saw Sara was awake, she hugged her arm. "Oh Sara, please stay awake. I want you to get better. You've been gone so long."

Linc, who had been staring out the window, walked over to the bed as soon as he heard Martha talking. "Sara, do you know you saved our lives? What you did was unbelievable!"

She replied that it was amazing what you could do when something horrible was about to happen.

"Martha, school's going to begin soon. Are you excited?"

"I started school this morning. Then we drove here to see you."

"You started school in Italy? I thought you were going home to Connecticut for school."

Martha started to laugh and began jumping up and down. "Oh Sara, you're so funny. You know we're not in Italy any more. We're home."

Linc quickly caught on to Sara's confused state. "You

have a lot of catching up to do," he informed her.

At that moment, Dad and Mom entered the room, arms loaded with flowers and an assortment of boxes. AJ followed, carrying a box obviously wrapped by his own fingers.

"I wrapped this all by myself," he announced.

"I know, and that makes it so much nicer. Thank you, AJ. Thank you. I can't wait to open everything."

There was so much to ask Gram, things that only Gram could answer. She would really like to talk with her alone again.

Everyone in the room seemed to overhear her silent plea. The look on their faces was comical. It was as if they were watching a favorite movie on TV and suddenly there was a power failure.

"Oh well, you're on again, Pat," Grandpa said as he nodded to Gram.

They filed out with expressions that seemed to say, "We just don't get it!"

They certainly weren't alone. Sara was totally confused as well.

Gram and Sara looked at each other. What an adventure the two had shared!

"Gram, please fill me in. Are we in Gaeta or Rome? Martha said she started school at home. If we are in the US, how did we get here?"

Before Gram got a chance to pull her chair next to Sara, two doctors entered the room.

Sara realized they were speaking English, with no sign of an Italian accent. They asked question after question about how she felt. Satisfied with her answers, they prescribed a little activity. She was to get up and really move around. They even said she might be able to go home in a few days, without any restrictions.

Great news! Now if more answers were forthcoming, the world might not be so topsy-turvy. A path back to reality would be most welcome.

As the doctors left, Gram pulled her chair close to Sara. "I'll continue where I left off, but please let me know if you get tired."

"Gram, I am so confused about everything. Nothing seems logical. Martha laughed when I mentioned we were in Italy. Where am I? How did I get here? Again, where were you when I came back from the Mt. Orlando tour? And after you tell me everything, have I got something to tell you!"

Gram began to laugh. "Sara, if it all weren't so serious, I'd say this would make a good movie, except no one would believe it! While you were on the tour, Vincent Albani, or rather someone pretending to be Vincent Albani, left a message at the front desk inviting us to dinner at his home. A car would pick us up around 5:00. I thought it would be appropriate to bring flowers to his house and went to that cute little florist near the inn to get some. I came back and put the flowers in the room. The florist had already put them in a vase filled with water. Then I went to sit out by that pretty garden at back. You know, it was where we sat before dinner one night."

Sara nodded. She did not want Gram to stop the story for anything.

"I was reading for a while when I noticed the man we'd seen on our way back from the café that morning—the one who was dressed so formally."

Another nod.

"He sat down a distance away and began reading the paper. After a few minutes, he came over to where I was sitting. I really wanted no part of a conversation, but there was no reason to be rude.

"He introduced himself. I had a hard time understanding him even though he spoke English, because his accent was so thick. I did manage to make out that he was a reporter for a travel magazine who was on an assignment exploring Gaeta for the magazine.

"When I got up to go inside, two men approached me.

137

I had no idea where they came from. It all happened so fast. One of the men pulled out a white cloth, and that is all I remember. Whatever was on that white cloth knocked me out cold. The gardener found me outside the toolshed when he went to get his shovel. I was taken to a hospital, where I finally awoke, but too late to help you.

"Fortunately, the gardener went to the garage shortly after he found me. He saw blood everywhere and noticed broken glass, spattered with blood, on the ground outside. When he looked into the garage, he found Simon lying there, bleeding profusely. The gardener immediately called the police.

"The police were unable to question Simon as he had lost consciousness, but before he came to, they were contacted by the Naval Base. You had been there, almost incoherent but able to alarm security that you were in a dangerous situation. The guard left you sitting in a chair while he called an ambulance and notified the police. It was only a short time before help arrived, but by then you had disappeared."

47 SARA GETS SOME ANSWERS

"I had to call our family. Sara, can you imagine what a horror that was? Martin, Anne, and Leanne came from Rome as soon as they heard. George was about to send his private jet to bring your mom and dad from home, but they had already purchased airline tickets to get there as quickly as possible. Luckily, they didn't have to leave home because you were found the same day, injured but, fortunately, alive.

"An Italian couple had gone to the police describing a young girl who had approached them. At first, they had thought she was drunk or a drug addict, but then she asked for a pen and wrote an address on their newspaper. They gave the police the article and the address. As I told you before, Martha and Linc's lives were saved because you left that message. They had been knocked out by chloroform but luckily had no injuries.

"The police found you lying on that bench, unconscious. You must have received a blow on the head because you had a concussion, in addition to a deep, infected cut on your arm and cuts all over your body.

"You were taken to a hospital in Gaeta. Even though you were unconscious, the doctors felt you could be flown home. We flew with the Balsams on their private jet. George remained at the Embassy with Anne. When we arrived in the US, you were taken by ambulance to St. Joseph's hospital, and that is where we are today—the same hospital where we took Grandpa when he was hit by the bicyclist.

"Oh, that phone call to the inn was not from Vincent Albani but from the terrorists imitating him. Those men knew everything about our plans."

"Gram, I understand now what happened, except you are wrong about where they found me. I went to sleep in Theresa's room, and that's the last I remember."

Sara described waking up in that building in pain. She included hearing the pitiful sounds of Martha and Linc.

"I know I escaped because there was a loud noise that caused the men to rush out, leaving the door open. I was so sick and in pain but I managed to get out. It was then that I approached that couple. I must have been a sight because they were petrified. I couldn't move from that bench for a while, and I guess I fell asleep. When I woke up, I felt so much better. My clothes were clean, and I didn't smell anymore.

"I walked, or rather ran, to 90 Indipendenze Plaza. I saw Theresa sitting at that little café across the street. We talked for a while. She saw how tired I was and invited me to go upstairs to her apartment with her. We sat down at a table that had a shiny cloth covering it. Her mother was cooking over the stove. It smelled so delicious. She told me it was called *brazol,* something like that. I had never heard that word before.

"Her mother made me a cup of espresso and invited me to stay for supper. I really didn't want to leave, but I knew I had to get back to our hotel and find you. I was so tired. They told me to rest in Theresa's bed. Theresa brought this pretty little bag in for me. She said she wanted me to have it so I would never forget her. I looked in the bag and it contained three lovely polished stones. Theresa said they were called *mare di vetro,* or 'sea of glass.' Gram, I even saw four sconces in their apartment!"

"Sara, what you are saying is unbelievable! The meal that she was making was called *braciole.* The shiny cloth on the table was probably oil cloth. They used to put it on kitchen tables. I have no idea how you know these things, but you never left the bench."

Sara was going to have to accept that Theresa was not real. Everything about her, the apartment, the furniture, and her mother were from another time. That saddened her, although she didn't know why. It was as if an event in her life that she deeply cared about had never happened. She began to cry.

"Sara, don't be unhappy. You're safe. Everyone's safe. We probably should never have taken that trip."

"Gram, are you kidding? Even with all the problems, I just had the greatest adventure of my life!"

"Oh, I almost forgot. What happened about the coins?" asked Sara, almost jumping out of bed when she thought about their "pirate treasure."

"Most of our suitcases are in my closet. I just gave one that had no coins to your mom. It had your passport and some clothes in it. The others haven't even been opened. I was so worried about you. Sharing the contents of our suitcases with the family will be our next adventure."

Sara wanted to go to the suitcases right away, rip the coins out of the hems of their clothes, and find out their value, but that would have to wait a few more days.

48 TIME HAS NO BOUNDARY

"There's something else, Gram. I know exactly what I want to do in life. I want to be a writer. Even if my time with the past wasn't real, I want to put those dreams into words.

"And I have one more question. Why is Anne Balsalm here? Why isn't she in Rome at the Embassy with her husband, George?"

"Sara, here's another chapter to include when you write this all down. Remember that Linc and Martha have an older brother, Quincy. He never made the trip with the family. A classmate of his stayed at the Balsam home with him because they both had summer jobs as lifeguards.

"As it turns out, this classmate was Simon's nephew. He and Quincy became good friends when they were freshman. Quincy is now a senior and last year, the two of them were roommates.

"I don't know the particulars, but Quincy shared all the information about the Embassy with his friend because Linc had emailed him every detail. Linc thought communicating with his brother was safe and couldn't possibly have any ramifications. He told Quincy not to talk about this with anyone.

"Quincy thought his roommate was above reproach, which he was. However, the roommate's uncle through marriage, Simon, was far from ethical. He had a connection with the foreign country causing the troubling situation overseas. When Simon found out his nephew had connections to a perfect source, he pressed him every day for news of the Embassy. The nephew thought nothing of this, as he and his uncle had always been close.

"So Linc shared everything that happened with his brother through emails, Quincy shared the news with his roommate, and the roommate shared the emails with Simon. That's how Simon knew exactly where we were.

"When the investigators in the US learned of this, they believed Quincy and his friend were involved. Anne is here to clear that all up. The family wants to keep this as quiet as possible. It certainly wouldn't look good if the Ambassador's grandson were involved in espionage, whether he is innocent or not. This whole episode is top secret. Our family knows this can't be discussed outside of those who are here.

"And now that you know everything, we'd better let our 'fans' in."

Their "fans" trooped in, looking anxiously at Sara. She wanted to let everyone know that she was fine and was now aware of all that had transpired.

"Linc, we've got a problem. We have a great story to tell when people ask us what we did on our summer vacation, but we have to squash it. I guess we'll just have to write about the Colosseum."

Everyone laughed, and the tension was broken. Mom and Dad came next to the bed and hugged her. AJ told Sara how much he loved her presents.

It was Mom who spoke next, changing Sara's life forever. "Sara, I emptied your suitcase last night and found this inside the case that contained your journal."

She handed Sara a tiny bag tied with a ribbon. The fabric of the bag was oh so familiar.

Martha saw something new and began her usual bouncing. "Open it, Sara!"

Gram sat right next to Sara, whose hands were shaking as she untied the ribbon and watched as three colored stones fell onto her sheet.

Everyone except Gram made some kind of casual remark about them and went on to another subject. Sara couldn't speak. All she could do was roll those precious pieces of glass over and over in her hands. Gram's eyes were wide with disbelief. They looked at each other without saying a word. Something unexplainable had happened. Time had crossed a line.

"Theresa, I will never forget you," Sara silently vowed.

49 NEVER UNDERESTIMATE THE POWER OF A WOMAN

Sara returned home from the hospital.

Gram removed the coins from their clothes.

They made a small fortune.

Taxes were hard to determine as the bounty was considered a gift, as truly it was.

Lawyers decided all was legal.

Every direct descendant of Theresa received an equal portion of the contents that were hidden for almost one hundred years. With the acquired fortune, Sara and her brother were able attend any college they wished. One cousin opened a luxurious pet kennel with a section for rescued dogs and cats. Another bought a gourmet restaurant that had been on the brink of bankruptcy and turned it into a five-star restaurant. He also managed a food mission where the hungry could be fed with the leftover food, topping each meal with a gourmet treat. One cousin built a company that guided tours to the most adventuresome locations in the world. He also spent a great deal of time and money bringing water and improving health conditions to Third World countries. Still another cousin created a daily television program whose sole purpose was to connect the needy with problem solvers who could help them. It became syndicated and was shown worldwide.

Theresa's descendants crossed the sea by ship to explore Gaeta. The family that had joined together for Sara's 15th birthday spent her 16th birthday at the villa near the Embassy as guests of and with the Balsalms.

Victor, the real-estate agent from Gaeta, received an anonymous $5,000 gift.

Gram and Sara had more adventures.

Why were the wrong sconces taken? This perplexing question was answered by one of Theresa's children who was still alive. Theresa's daughter, Gloria, now 90 years old, spoke of the conversations she had heard between her mother and her grandmother when she was a child. They often talked about the unfortunate arrival of the wrong sconces.

Theresa, her mother, and her brother were on a waiting list for passenger space. They had collected enough money to purchase three tickets for America, and they were being sponsored by several relatives in America, including Theresa's father. The three went to the immigration office to obtain their passports. There was no problem obtaining them; the woman who issued the passports was most helpful.

They discovered that a ship leaving in two days had three seats available. The news was coming across on a method of communication called a ticker tape. The next availability would be many weeks away. That was too long for a family wanting to start a new life, so the three of them rushed to a travel agent office and purchased their tickets.

A lifetime of possessions had to be packed in only a few days or left behind because the luggage they could take was limited. Within a day everything was sorted. They gave all their furniture to relatives. They also asked an uncle to remove two of the sconces, fix the wall, pack the sconces, and send them to the address of their new home. Theresa's mother left him the money for that transaction. Unfortunately, the uncle removed the wrong sconces. After that, the landlord wouldn't let anyone into that apartment. Theresa's family suspected that he had discovered the treasure and confiscated it. They felt it was lost to the family forever.

Not true.

The bag that held all the money contained envelopes that Theresa's father and brother had sent from America. One envelope contained an unused stamp that Theresa's brother had sent to her, which now was worth a fortune. It was a one cent US stamp in which Washington's picture was reversed. The brother sent it to her as a joke. He thought it was worthless.

Not so!

It had been Sara's idea to use a hairdryer to dry and protect the papers. Our girl turned out to be quite the heroine—from saving lives to saving a fortune.

WHAT A GIRL!

ABOUT THE AUTHORS

PJ Dischino calls herself a Grandma Moses author. She celebrated her 80th birthday by engaging her 15-year-old granddaughter to create an action-packed novel geared toward teens.

The dream to write a novel has always been a "what if" for PJ. The dream started to become a reality while she was sitting at a pool with her granddaughter, Sara, one day. FaceTime connected the two every weekend for a year. Stevie, another teen, drew the sea glass illustration for the book. Thus, the young and the old have combined their talents here to create an adventure full of mystery and intrigue.

18138029R00096

Made in the USA
Middletown, DE
26 February 2015